SPACERS
FIRST 1 COMMAND

MIRTH PUBLISHING
ST. JOHN'S

SCOTT BARTLETT

Library and Archives Canada Cataloguing in Publication

Bartlett, Scott

First Command / Scott Bartlett ; illustrations by Tom Edwards ; typography and interior formatting by Steve Beaulieu.

ISBN 978-1-988380-17-9

To Lawrence Tate — thank you for your incredible support of my writing.

CHAPTER ONE

Aboard the *New Jersey*
Elsin System, Tempore Region
Earth Year 2290

"What do you have for me, Lucy?" Captain Alfred Vaughn asked, turning toward the operations officer seated to his left, a few feet below the raised captain's chair. He could tell from the nervous way the lieutenant tapped at her console that she had something to report.

"The *Squall* just jumped in from the Olent Region, sir," Lucy Guerrero said. "I've already parsed her report, if you're ready to hear it."

Al nodded, concealing a grin at Lucy's polished words. She might be jumpy, but he doubted there was a more competent operations officer in all of Frontier Security. Hell, he'd probably be jumpy too, in her position: the sole breadwinner for two toddlers and a stay-at-home husband living back on Oasis Colony. How that man could bear it while his wife risked life and limb in the Contested Regions, Al didn't know, but he supposed it wasn't his business.

"*Squall* says there's a known pirate scow in the first Olent System, Captain. It's orbiting a gas giant's moon less than fifty thousand kilometers from the regional jump zone. It appears to be alone."

Billy Candle twisted in the XO's chair, a gleam in his eye. "Could be they have a hidden stash on that moon."

"Indeed they could, Billy," Al answered. Like all Frontier crews, the men and women serving aboard the *New Jersey* would get twenty percent of the value of all stolen goods they recovered, to be portioned out according to rank and seniority. Al was on his way to becoming a millionaire, and he'd earned more for his crew than any other ship in company history. That was why his people were so covetous of their positions aboard his command.

But it never paid to be reckless.

"Or," he continued, "they might just be idling, waiting for other pirates to join up with them for a raid. We proceed with caution. Is that clear?"

"Clear, sir," Billy said. But Al could still hear the hunger in his voice.

"Good. Nav, set a course for the Olent jump gate and send it to Helm. Maintain cruising speed." *No need to waste fuel by accelerating,* he figured. "Tell the *Squall* to come with us—we may need her electronic warfare suite."

"Aye," both the Nav and Helm officers answered.

Strange rumors had been coming out of the far north, lately. Tales of pirates banding together, even some particularly outlandish stories of them trying to form their own corporations. Which was ridiculous. The UNC would send out their superships at the first whiff of something like that, making piracy a business model that just wouldn't scale in the Dawn Cluster. No matter how far from Earth the Cluster was located.

As much as everyone resented the United Nations and

Colonies—their meddlesome ways; how they limited the number of non-UNC warships and withheld vital technologies, for 'the good of all'—Al had to admit their presence did afford a certain level of stability. It wasn't just the handful of hulking super-ships they kept in the Cluster, either. No, the biggest thing keeping everyone honest was the widespread knowledge that, at the first sign of misbehavior, the UNC could and would bring nearly limitless numbers of ships through the wormhole connecting the Dawn Cluster to Earth.

To the UNC, "misbehavior" was a broad term. They placed strict limits on how large any given corporate military was allowed to grow, for example. They also didn't allow any fighting between the thousands of corps operating in the Dawn Cluster. Skirmishes still happened, of course, but the UNC usually found out, and stiff penalties came fast and hard.

Doesn't matter much to me, Al thought. He had no interest in fighting other corporations, and though he resented the UNC as much as the next guy, he did like their standardized regulations for the redistribution of recovered stolen goods. Fifty percent to the original owner, thirty percent to the corp that bore the cost and risk of recovering the goods, and twenty percent to the captain and crew who put their lives on the line to do the recovering.

He jerked his arm up and coughed into the inside of his elbow before replacing it on his chair's armrest. As he did, he noticed his XO studying him with a concerned look from the station just ahead of his.

"What?" Al said.

"You all right, Skipper?"

Al's jaw tightened as he cast covert glances at his Ops and Tactical officers, to see whether they would react to Billy's question. He lowered his voice to a growl. "Ask me that one more time and I'll have you lashed to the *New Jersey*'s prow."

"Yes, sir," the lieutenant commander said.

Lowering his voice in the hopes the rest of the CIC crew wouldn't hear, Al said, "It's my ticker that's the problem, not a cough, Billy. Besides, they cleared me for duty."

"I know it." The XO didn't sound very convinced.

Al didn't blame Billy for being doubtful. Serving under a captain who'd suffered a heart attack two short months ago probably didn't inspire much confidence, especially considering how hastily Frontier Security's medical personnel had put him back in action after sticking a pacemaker in him.

But the northern regions were becoming heated in recent months, and Al got the sense things could boil over any day now. Frontier needed all hands on deck. Besides, he was glad to be back in the captain's chair. There was nowhere he'd rather be than sailing through hot-zone star systems, shooting down pirates and getting rich.

"Approaching the jump gate now, sir," Billy said. "Engineering reports the inertial compensators passed their checks. Shields are lowered, and the *Jersey*'s ready to jump."

Al nodded, then eyed his operations officer. "Lucy?"

"The gate appears fully functional, captain. Zero structural damage, and energy readings are all coming back green."

"Okay," he said, but still didn't give the order to jump. Instead, he called up a zoomed-in visual of the jump gate on his holoscreen and studied it. Call it superstition, but he always liked to eyeball gates before using them. The chances of noticing a problem from visual inspection were small, but too many ships had been torn apart by faulty jump gates. So he liked to have a look for himself.

Being a gate that connected two regions—Tempore and Olent—this gate was larger than most. It consisted of three mammoth rings, each bigger than the last, all lit by a soft, solar-powered blue glow. Using a jump gate was like being fired from a gun. And he didn't enjoy being the round fired.

"Go ahead, Helm. Take us through."

"Aye, sir," Lieutenant Randall Kitt said.

The *New Jersey* coasted into the first ring and suddenly lurched forward with a force that never failed to startle Al. His heart skipped a beat, and he winced, resisting the urge to place a hand over his chest.

Even with the inertial compensators, the forward thrust shoved him back into the captain's chair like a giant's palm pressing against him. *This can't be good for a man with an unreliable ticker,* he thought. But he'd never let his dislike of jumping deter him before, and he wouldn't now.

His holoscreen still showed an exterior visual, and he watched as the universe coalesced into a tunnel of solid gray, the starlight washed out by the void and the ship's speed.

After what seemed an eternity, but was actually less than a minute, the ship emerged into the destination system, having traversed the better part of a light year.

"There's the pirate scow," Lucy said as her threat board populated. "Orbiting a gas giant's moon, just as the *Squall* said."

Al's eyes were on the 3D display inside the holographic tank at the front of the CIC. The display could be zoomed in to encompass just the two ships or zoomed out to show the entire star system. The fact the scow was still in the moon's orbit suggested Billy's theory might be right: they could be stowing booty there from a recent raid. If the pirates really did have the nerve to secret a stash on that moon's surface, Al and his CIC crew might be on the verge of becoming ridiculously wealthy. *I could be on my way to retirement. Give this old ticker of mine a rest.*

On the other hand, this could be a trap. That didn't scare him too much—he'd intentionally sprung plenty of pirate traps before, only to destroy the tub whose captain thought he'd gotten the upper hand. But caution usually paid off.

"Run full active scans of that moon and the space around it, Lucy," he said.

"Aye, sir."

The powerful scans would amount to lighting a beacon on a hilltop for any other ships in-system, but at this range, the pirate ship had almost certainly seen the *Jersey* anyway.

"Randy, reverse thrust until we've cut our speed in half. I don't want to blunder into anything nasty."

"Aye," the Helm officer said in his soft-spoken way.

"Sir, can I recommend a more aggressive approach?" Billy spoke slightly faster than before. "It's just one ship."

"We'll maintain our present speed, XO." He could tell Billy would rather plunge headlong into battle, deal with the scow, and reap the rewards. The XO was always nudging Al to take on more risk, knowing it would lead to greater rewards. Always encouraging him to go just one system deeper, to engage one pirate ship more. Al was able to keep him in check, but he'd raised an eyebrow at the XO's overeagerness more than once. What made the man so money-hungry? A gambling addiction, kept at bay only by these long patrols? Or something else? Debt, perhaps?

"The scans aren't turning up anything, sir," Lucy said. "As far as I can see, that space is clear, along with the rest of the system. I can only see that one ship."

"Let's get 'em," Billy said. "This is gonna be the big one, Skipper. I can taste it."

"All right," Al said reluctantly. "Helm, bring us to seventy-five percent thrust and maintain acceleration until I say so. Billy, have the missile bay crew load an Ogre into the tube."

"With pleasure." Billy's voice all but vibrated with excitement.

"Lucy," Al said, and the operations officer glanced at him. "Has that thing put up a shield?"

"Negative, Captain."

"Good." It wasn't uncommon for pirates to mismanage their energy resources so badly they lacked enough to power their shields. Plenty of pirate scows didn't even have shields. Either way, a single well-placed Ogre should be enough to turn this tub to slag. "XO, tell our forward gunners to get ready to engage, in case the target does manage to put up a force field."

"Aye, Skipper," Billy said, though a measure of uncertainty had crept into his voice.

Probably because I called him XO, and not Billy. But he'd done it for a reason: to remind Billy that, when it came to engaging an enemy, professionalism would always carry the day over bravado. *Or greed.*

He knew that, intellectually. But in practice, he knew he often succumbed to the same temptations Billy did.

Lucy shifted at her console. "Entering Ogre firing range."

Then let's not give them any more time than we need to. "Fire at will, Tactical."

Lieutenant Tim Ortega nodded. "Firing Ogre."

The ship rumbled as the heavy missile sprang from the *New Jersey*'s only missile tube, rocketing through space on a jet of vaporizing fuel. Ogres were notoriously difficult to evade. Once one had a lock, it would pursue its target relentlessly until striking home or running out of fuel. Typically, the former happened long before the latter could.

"Sir." The tension in Lucy's voice made Al look up sharply. "We…my God. We have a problem, sir."

"What is it?" He ignored the tightening sensation in his chest.

"Multiple enemy contacts. Six of them, rising from the gas giant's clouds."

Al felt his eyes go wide. He hadn't even considered that something might be hiding inside the gas giant itself—certainly

SCOTT BARTLETT

not a force big enough to pose a meaningful threat. Pirates just didn't have that kind of numbers. Except, there they were, clear as day in the holotank, and clearly operating together. *That shouldn't be. They must know the UNC won't let them organize like this for long.*

For the moment, none of that mattered. What did matter was that they were hurtling toward an enemy that outnumbered them seven-to-one.

"Helm, reverse thrust, engines at one hundred percent."

"Reversing thrust now, Captain."

The maneuver tossed Al forward, his restraints biting into his chest. Then the inertial compensators kicked in, and he settled back into his seat.

But Lucy had more bad news for him. "Sir, the scow just activated a shield."

Damn it. That would minimize the Ogre's impact. Missiles weren't very effective when it came to knocking down shields.

But Lucy wasn't finished. "Captain, the..." Again, she seemed momentarily lost for words. "Our missile. It's...turning around."

"Turning *around?*" Al repeated in disbelief. Was Lucy making some sick joke?

"Toward us, sir. It's headed straight toward us. So are the pirate ships—all seven of them are accelerating at top speed."

"Shields, Tim."

"Aye, sir. Activating them now."

The shimmering energy field came up just in time to catch the Ogre, its fiery impact skittering across the transparent shell before burning out in the void.

Lucy Guerrero spoke again, sounding tenser than ever. "Sir, I'm getting readings on a new contact, rising out of the gas giant beyond the pirate formation. It's huge."

"How huge?" Al asked. "UNC super-ship huge?"

8

Guerrero met his gaze. "I don't think it's of human make, sir."

"Get me a visual."

The ship that appeared on his holoscreen was indeed enormous, with two long projections like pincers that pointed straight at the *New Jersey*. A great ring graced the strange vessel's rear, with fins jutting off it in four directions.

"We're disengaging. Billy, have the missile crews load up another Ogre, and then another as soon as it's fired. We'll need them to cover our escape."

"They've already loaded one. But sir, what if the Ogres turn around on us again? What if that vessel is the reason it's happening?"

Al blinked. His chest felt tight, and he realized he was panicking. At least, *something* was fogging up his thoughts. He shook himself. "For now, we're assuming that was a gross malfunction at the worst possible time. If that wasn't the case, then I'm not sure how we're getting out of this."

"Understood, sir. Who should we target?"

"The same ship as before." The fog was receding from his mind, and he saw something he'd been missing: his missiles wouldn't get through to the target until he took down its shields. It was pointless to launch until he had a decent chance of hitting a hull. "Wait. Lucy, is the target within firing range of our primary laser?"

"It is, sir."

"Okay. Tim, coordinate with Helm to target that ship with the primary, just long enough to take down its shield. But first, fire the Ogre." That would minimize the target's reaction time. He needed to start wiping threats from the battlespace.

"Firing Ogre," Ortega said. The *Jersey* shuddered as he let the missile fly. "Now firing primary."

The ship trembled again as her main capacitor came alive,

powering the mighty beam that lanced through space to strike the target's shield.

Lucy twisted toward him. "The target's shield is down."

"Good. Use the next Ogre on another target, Tim. I'll let you determine the most viable one."

Al took a breath, trying to ignore the questions hammering on the door of his brain. Was Lucy right about that behemoth belonging to aliens? The only intelligent species humanity had ever encountered were the Xanthic. But they'd only ever attacked Earth. What would they be doing in the Dawn Cluster— and how did they get here without anyone between here and the wormhole noticing them?

And, perhaps most horrifying of all: why were they working with human pirates?

Forget about that for now, he scolded himself. *As long as we keep our heads, we'll get out of here in one piece.* No pirate force was going to take out the *New Jersey.* Not even one backed up by a Xanthic battleship.

"The pirates have entered laser range and are firing," Lucy said. "Our shield is taking a beating, sir. Their main lasers are weak, but our force field won't stand up to all seven of them for very long."

Al felt himself tense as he watched his missiles sail across the intervening space, wishing that Veronica Rose, Frontier's CEO, had seen fit to assign even a single logistics ship to fly with him.

I just need to start cutting down their numbers. If I can do that soon, we'll be able to escape.

Then, Lucy's body went rigid. "Sir. The Ogres are turning again. They're headed back toward us."

Al stared wordlessly at the holotank. *Impossible. It shouldn't be possible.* But it *was* happening, and the alien craft clearly had something to do with it.

"Our shields just went down, sir."

A wave of fatigue crashed over Al, and his chest tightened again, more sharply than before. "I can't breathe," he gasped, collapsing forward into his restraints as his vision blurred.

Billy Candle was clawing at his own restraints, freeing himself from the XO's chair as he yelled for someone to get a medic. Lucy just stared at him from her console, her mouth open. The last thing Al saw was how white her face had become.

CHAPTER TWO

Norfolk, Virginia
Sol System, Earth Local Space
Earth Year 2290

IN TAD THATCHER'S EXPERIENCE, EXECUTIVE OFFICERS WERE about as busy as they made themselves. He'd had XOs who never stopped in their mission to make sure their ships ran as efficiently as possible, acting as a sort of force multiplier for the captain's authority. He'd also had XOs he barely knew were part of the unit, since they managed to weasel their way out of having any real responsibility—although Thatcher considered those situations just as much the captain's fault as the XO's.

As XO of the USS *Hepburn*, Tad Thatcher kept himself busy. So busy, in fact, that he found himself putting together a new drill schedule in his upstairs office, when he should have been downstairs enjoying home leave with his pregnant wife.

This should only take a couple more hours. Then there's the exercise plan Captain Wilcox wants me to put together for the marines, but that can wait till tomorrow...

He liked to keep the news on while he worked, even aboard

the *Hepburn*—he'd download the latest in 24-hour chunks and play it while putting together an inspection report or assigning Engineering personnel to handle the next routine reactor shutdown.

This wasn't to keep up on the daily happenings throughout UNC-controlled space, however. Far from it. No, he simply worked fastest with someone talking in the background. He didn't know why, but he'd always been that way.

And of course, the best sort of background talking was the kind he could safely ignore. Any of the largest news outlets fit that bill nicely. Almost without fail, they prattled on endlessly about things that failed either to convince or compel Tad Thatcher.

By definition, for something to count as "news" it had to be something that almost never happened, so Thatcher could count on the news to always tell him things that were very, very unlikely to ever concern him. And the way modern news outlets sensationalized everything, trying their best to inflame their viewers and listeners—that only made Thatcher feel safer in ignoring it. It was, by and large, trash.

Today was different, though. Today, Thatcher found himself looking up from his work, staring at the white, rounded speaker sitting on his desk as the newsman told him something that would change his life forever, along with the lives of every living human.

"We interrupt this broadcast to bring you some unsettling news from the planet Barton. The colony there has been completely overwhelmed by Xanthic troopers. These troopers were not brought by a fleet superior to ours, as we have always feared. Instead, they seemed to emerge from under the ground, boiling up from cave and sewer systems to brutalize the civilian population living on the planet's surface."

The Xanthic. They're back. It had been hearing his grandfather's stories of fighting the Xanthic fleet fifty years ago that had led Thatcher to join the U.S. Space Fleet, with the dream of one day commanding his own warship. His grandfather's generation had forced the Xanthic back, but not before they laid waste to seven human colonies. Now, it seemed they'd added an eighth.

"After comparing images of the aliens attacking Barton with the bodies recovered from wrecked Xanthic ships in the past," the newscaster went on, "xenobiologists say they're certain they belong to the same species."

Thatcher drew a hand over the mustache and beard that had been growing since he returned to Earth, and he suppressed a shudder. His grandfather, Edward Thatcher, had been one of those to board a Xanthic craft. When he judged Tad was old enough, and he saw his grandson was serious about joining the Fleet, he started sharing the darker details from the war, so that Tad would be prepared if he ever had to face the Xanthic.

Edward couldn't share everything, since he was sworn to secrecy—in particular, Thatcher noticed his grandfather never gave any details about the Xanthic ship he'd boarded. But one detail he did divulge was how the surviving Xanthic crewmembers had all suicided, drawing their scythe-like forearms across their own respiratory tracts. *They must have known what we'd do to them.*

"Kathy Hong, a leading xenopathologist, has pointed out that Barton is located in one of the star systems affected by the interstellar gas cloud that enveloped local space three years ago. The nature of the cloud has been a topic hotly debated in the scientific community ever since it abruptly dissipated within a few weeks of its arrival. Now, Hong is proposing a new theory: the cloud was a transmission medium for Xanthic genetic material, which it deposited in underground reservoirs suitable for their incubation. Hong's peers are calling the theory wildly speculative, but alternative explanations are sorely lacking as experts scramble to—"

"Stop broadcast," Thatcher said, and the speaker cut off. He couldn't tell whether tying in the gas cloud was just the newscaster's attempt to make the public even more afraid than they were going to be. To make sure they kept paying attention to the news. At the time, the arrival of the interstellar gas cloud *had* been frightening. Astronomers warned the cloud was dense enough to cool planets. Worse, the dust and gas would infiltrate the upper atmospheres of habitable planets, eating away at the oxygen there. But the true doomsday scenario had come from their prediction that the gas cloud would arrest the solar wind that naturally flowed within each star system, protecting planetary lifeforms (like humans) from the high-speed electrons and ions that tear constantly through space. Without the solar wind to usher them away, they would rip into planetary atmospheres, and then into the molecules that made up the life on those planets.

Except, none of that happened. The interstellar gas cloud that arrived proved extremely unusual—in its size and the speed of its movement, but also in the fact that it dissipated so fast. Yes, some of the effects the astronomers warned about took place, but after the cloud's disappearance everything quickly went back to normal.

Thatcher pushed himself up from his desk and crossed the office, forcing himself to walk with a measured stride, and to refrain from yanking the door open. He headed downstairs to find his wife with her Lenses pushed up onto her head. She was leaning forward, keyboard folded and dangling between her legs as she stared into space.

"Lin," Thatcher said, standing uncertainly in the doorway. "You heard the news?"

His wife's almond eyes met his, her mouth forming the perfect "O" it made when she was distressed. Without a word, she got up, her straight black hair swaying as she crossed the room to embrace him. He hugged her back, intensely aware of the firm lump that pressed against his abdomen, where their son was growing.

"Elise just texted me," she said. "The Xanthic." Head tilting up, she stared into his eyes. "You'll be deployed again, won't you? Before your home leave ends."

He hesitated, then nodded. "Probably any day now."

She continued to stare into him, and he knew what was going through her mind. His enlistment date was coming up soon. If he didn't re-up, then he'd be home with her and their baby. He'd be safe.

Unless the Xanthic bring the war all the way to Earth. Unless they win.

He knew Lin wouldn't ask him not to reenlist. Not when he still hadn't achieved his dream of commanding a warship. Not when humanity so clearly needed him.

But she was thinking it. He could see it in her beautiful brown eyes.

His Lenses buzzed, and he slipped them out of his breast pocket, unfolding them and putting them on.

"I'm being called into base," Thatcher said, frowning. The message didn't say to prepare for deployment—it just said to report to Rear Admiral Faulkner of the U.S. Space Fleet Forces Command at the Hampton Roads Naval base.

It's obviously something to do with the Xanthic. But why aren't I being deployed?

He'd find out soon enough. And he had a feeling he wouldn't like it.

CHAPTER THREE

Hampton Roads Naval Support Base
Sol System, Earth Local Space
Earth Year 2290

WHAT OTHER SURPRISES CAN TODAY POSSIBLY BRING?

As Thatcher marched briskly toward his superior's office, black boots clicking smartly on polished tile, he was still puzzling over the reason a rear admiral would want to meet with him specifically.

The admiral's staff car had whisked him from his house and through the base's security checkpoints. He'd sat in the back of the empty car for the ten-minute ride, his fingers laced between his knees, as he stared out the front window and lost himself in thought.

He enjoyed the commute to and from the base, and he often wished it were longer. People who complained about commute times baffled him. That was when he got his best thinking done —when the answer to some problem that had long been nagging him would pop into his head.

He could have taken his own car to the base, but why do that when the admiral had offered his staff car? Things were expensive enough on Earth without turning down what assistance his employer offered. The U.S. Space Fleet liked having its personnel on humanity's home planet, which had become the New York City of local space when it came to the cost of living. As for NYC itself—well, he'd have to go private military for a hope of affording that. *I'd probably need to own my own firm.* Neither of those seemed likely to happen anytime soon.

Besides, who wants to live there?

If he was being honest with himself, planetside life made him restless in general. He was the polar opposite of most spacers, who were drawn to the Fleet by the promise of adventure, of traversing the stars and learning their secrets—only to learn that life in space was mostly cramped, cold, and boring.

But Thatcher liked the simplicity, and the routine, of spacer life. Strangely, the tight framework imposed by space gave him a sense of ultimate freedom. The sense that what he did truly mattered, and that the fates of his ship and her crew were intimately bound up with how well he performed each task.

He'd felt that way even as a junior officer fresh from training.

He rapped smartly on the office door, just below the plaque that read "REAR ADMIRAL ZEBEDIAH FAULKNER." A voice called for him to come in.

Entering, Thatcher found Admiral Faulkner sitting behind his desk, which was bare other than a keyboard connected to a pair of Lenses folded neatly beside it, and a mug of steaming coffee sitting on a granite coaster. Another mug sat in front of a man wearing a business suit, who twisted in his seat to smile at Thatcher, revealing a scarlet tie. His attire contrasted with the admiral, who wore a navy-blue cardigan with epaulet tabs that displayed his two stars.

Thatcher tried not to eye the man in the suit. *Who could smile on a day like today?*

"At ease, Commander," Faulkner said as Thatcher came to attention, saluting. "Please, have a seat. Can I get you a mug?"

"No thank you, sir." Thatcher sat.

"Down to business, then. I'm sure you've heard the news about the Xanthic, and you must be wondering why you received a message to meet with me, instead of deployment orders."

"The thought had crossed my mind, sir," Thatcher said, again suppressing the urge to glance curiously at the man sitting beside him.

"Commander, meet Chief Petty Officer Lionel O'Malley, from Frontier Security."

Grin widening, O'Malley offered his hand, and Thatcher gripped it, pumping it twice. "Pleased to meet you, Commander," O'Malley said, speaking with a light Irish accent. He didn't call Thatcher "sir," since they weren't part of the same military structure, as much as private military companies tried to pretend they were. Thatcher was glad O'Malley didn't. He would have been insulted if the man had pretended that to his face.

"And you," Thatcher said. He wasn't disdainful of private militaries, exactly. Plenty of good friends had chosen to join their ranks instead of re-upping, in exchange for a salary that more than doubled what the Fleet could pay.

Thatcher had gotten no shortage of job offers himself, especially as his enlistment date approached. But he'd turned them all down. He hadn't become a spacer of the U.S. Space Fleet to make money. The mere idea of that was laughable. He'd joined because he wanted to serve his country and to protect her people. To safeguard what few liberties the UNC, with their widespread surveillance and daily little indignities, had left them.

Just as his grandfather had.

"Commander," Faulkner said, "we've known about the attack on Barton longer than the media has. Barely twenty-four hours longer, but long enough to start taking some action. The Xanthic's sudden appearance has put us in a…strange position. And it's pushed us to take some strange actions."

Thatcher nodded, and waited, unsure what to say. Beside him, O'Malley seemed somewhat tense, though he was clearly striving to look relaxed.

"Lionel here is a recruiter for Frontier," the admiral said at last.

Blinking, Thatcher stared back at his superior, dumbstruck. *So. This is just another job offer. But why is it happening in front of a flag officer?*

"I know this must seem highly unusual to you, like I already said. Trust me, I never thought I'd be in the position of encouraging a Fleet officer to join a PMC. Personally, I've never liked the way they piggyback off our recruitment efforts, picking off our trained personnel without ever having to invest in training themselves."

O'Malley shifted in his seat.

"Nevertheless," the admiral went on. "Frontier is part of a corporate alliance called the Oasis Protectorate, responsible for servicing and defending America's premiere colony in the Dawn Cluster. Lately, increased pirate activity in the Cluster's northern regions has complicated their job. It seems the pirates are banding together like they never have before. And a recent incident has led us to believe that things in the star cluster may be about to get just as interesting as they got for Earth Local Space."

"What incident, sir?"

"Thatcher, you must not repeat what I'm about to tell you, under pain of treason. Do you understand?"

Thatcher's eyes never left the admiral's as his stomach slowly sank toward his feet. "Yes, sir."

"A Frontier ship—a Griffon-class light armored cruiser, called the *New Jersey*—was just attacked in the Tempore Region by a battle group consisting of seven pirate ships and an eighth vessel which we have good reason to believe was an advanced Xanthic craft."

The admiral paused, and Thatcher sat perfectly still.

Apparently satisfied that he'd absorbed the news, the admiral continued. "I'm sure you can appreciate that if this got out, it would destabilize the Dawn Cluster in a way humanity can't afford right now, teetering on the brink of war as we are. The alien craft the *New Jersey* faced had the ability to turn the cruiser's own missiles against her. During the engagement, Frontier lost their best captain, Alfred Vaughn, to a heart attack. His XO was able to take command and get them out of there, though the cruiser was heavily damaged and is currently undergoing repairs. The company needs a replacement captain for Vaughn."

A thrill shot through Thatcher's chest, and he noticed his breath deepening. It was a strange sensation, next to the dread Faulkner's words had caused him.

The admiral nodded, as though Thatcher had spoken his excitement out loud. "With the way the UNC limits the number of ships we can field, you're years from receiving your first command—in the Fleet. But I know you're more than ready, Commander. And if you accept an offer from Frontier, you could be captaining your first ship by the end of the month."

"You'd need to challenge some aptitude tests," O'Malley put in. "The Ogre and Hellborn missile school exams, as well as tests on the ship's engineering plant, shiphandling, tactics, interstellar law, leadership, safety, communications, and...well, a lot of other things."

"He can do that en route to the Dawn Cluster," Faulkner said. "If the glowing report his direct superior gave is any indication, Thatcher will barely need to study."

"I'd need to study some," Thatcher said, a little haltingly. "But...I'm still not sure I understand this, sir."

"You're still wondering why I'm encouraging you to take a

PMC job? Or why I'm encouraging you to take this particular posting as ship captain?"

"Both, I guess."

"There aren't very many spacers coming up on their enlistment dates who are ship-captain material, Commander. To be honest, I consider it a stroke of luck that you're one of them, and Command has agreed to shave the final weeks off your enlistment. As for why I'd cooperate with Frontier in the poaching of one of our finest...Commander, the Fleet has no presence in the Dawn Cluster, and with the Xanthic returning to Earth Local Space, the UNC won't have the ships to devote to ensuring the Cluster remains stable. But it *must* remain stable, Commander. If we're going to fund a prolonged war against the Xanthic, a strong, stable Dawn Cluster is going to be vital."

Slowly, Thatcher nodded. Ever since humanity had managed to tease open the wormhole connecting the Cluster to Earth Space, and to stabilize it, humanity had reaped the rewards of the unusually dense, unusually resource-laden star cluster. Over the last century, it had become the primary engine of industry, and corporations had flooded in to stake their claim and harvest those resources, building business empires that indirectly enriched the species as a whole.

"We need you to go to Tempore and find out why human pirates are working with the Xanthic—and also just how many enemy craft are lurking in the Cluster's northern Contested Regions. We need a calm, productive Dawn Cluster, Thatcher. If you can help us achieve that, you'll be serving not just the United States but all of humanity. Besides, Frontier is an all American company. By all reports, serving on one of their ships is virtually identical to serving on one of ours."

Thatcher drew a deep breath, then another. His gaze drifted to O'Malley, remained there for several seconds, then returned to Faulkner.

"I'll need some time to think about it, sir. To talk it over with my wife."

"I can give you five hours."

Raising his eyebrows, Thatcher opened his mouth, then closed it again. *Five hours.* "Yes, sir. I understand."

CHAPTER FOUR

Hampton Roads Spaceport
Sol System, Earth Local Space
Earth Year 2290

LIN'S ARMS WERE TIGHT AROUND HIM ONCE MORE, HER protruding stomach a solid reminder of exactly what he was leaving behind.

She'd gone through spaceport security with him—they allowed her to go through the same expedited screening he had, even though she wasn't strictly eligible. It wasn't the first time someone had bent the rules because he was a service member. The U.S. military had allowed itself to become a shadow of its former self, but its members were still fiercely proud, and their nation still proudly supported them. For the most part.

"I'm glad you're going," Lin whispered against his chest as they stood outside the boarding bridge for the shuttle slated to take him into orbit.

He pulled back a little. "Huh? You're...glad?"

"To the Dawn Cluster, I mean. You'd be going anyway, but

you'll be safer in the Cluster. I'd put you up against a few raggedy pirates any day, but the Xanthic...." She shivered.

Thatcher tried not to wince. Officially, his reason for going to the Dawn Cluster was to investigate why pirates were banding together in unprecedented numbers. He hadn't been able to mention the Xanthic's appearance there to anyone. Including Lin.

Now, she pressed her face against his uniform and began to sob quietly.

"Lin? What is it?"

"You'll miss the birth. And all the 'first times' for our son. His first steps. Maybe even his first words..."

"I want you to record them for me. Never stop recording. That way, I won't miss them. And I'll always be with you, Lin. Even when I'm not here. Remember that." He kissed the top of her head.

She lifted her face from the damp blotch she'd made to peer up at him. "I won't know you the same, when you come back. I'll be shy again. Like last time."

He smiled, remembering how nervous and awkward Lin had been when he'd returned from his last deployment. It was the kind of endearing quirk that had made him fall in love with her in the first place. "I'll write every day, sweetheart. I'll send videos. You'll know me just as well as you do now."

"Okay, Tad. I love you."

"I love you, too."

When he first told her about Frontier's offer, she'd gotten distraught at the idea of him traveling so far away—tens of thousands of light years away, technically. But the higher salary would help them to continue calling Earth their home, even to save for their son's education. They'd remain on the same planet as both their parents. True, their parents lived in Nebraska, but there'd be nothing stopping Lin from moving there, now. Even if she stayed in Virginia, it was much better to be a few states away than a few star systems.

Before they parted for the last time, Lin said, "What will we name him?"

"Hmm? Oh. We still haven't decided, have we?"

She shook her head.

"What do you think we should name him?"

"Edward. For your grandfather."

Thatcher felt a smile stretch his cheeks wide. It delighted him that she'd been the one to suggest it. It was what he'd wanted all along, of course. "We'll name him Edward," he said.

Two hours later, the shuttle docked with the *Goliath,* a freighter that did regular cargo runs from the Dawn Cluster's Clime Region to the Sol System. The shuttle was packed with passengers headed for the Cluster—all civilians, except for Thatcher. New and long-time workers for one of the thousands of corporations operating in the Cluster, mostly, though some were probably colonists. A couple had gotten sick during the rough ride through Earth's atmosphere, but luckily they'd found their vomit bags in time.

As everyone lined up to scan their boarding passes and wait for the cargo hold to spit their luggage down the chute near the airlock, a man with a thick Southern accent started shouting.

"Hey! Excuse me! Let's let these service men go to the front, people. Come on, now. Clear a path. It's the least we can do, am I right?"

Thatcher smiled faintly as the shuttle's passengers drew aside, clearing the way for him. *Service men? I didn't know someone else was military on here. Must have been sitting near the back.* "Thank you," he murmured as he carefully made his way past the shuttle passengers. "Thank you."

He reached the open airlock—since the shuttle had docked directly with the *Goliath,* there was no need for it to cycle—and scanned his pass. The hold spat out his large duffel bag within a few seconds. It wasn't uncommon for the system to keep a military member's luggage near the front, for easy access.

Bag in hand, he waited outside the shuttle to greet the other service member, and was pleasantly surprised when a young man wearing a Fleet uniform emerged. Even holding his own bag, he managed to come smartly to attention, executing a crisp salute.

"At ease, Ensign." Thatcher stuck out his hand. "I'm Tad Thatcher. Please, call me Tad."

"Nice to meet you, uh, Tad. I'm Jimmy Devine." The lad smiled, but Thatcher could tell he was intimidated. *By my rank, or my personality?* Thatcher knew he could be intimidating when he wanted to be, but right now he wasn't trying.

"Listen, before we get settled away in our cabins, why don't we get a drink? On the trip up I read that the *Goliath* has a well-stocked taproom." Thatcher wasn't much of a drinker, but he had learned that sharing a beer was a good way to put a lower-ranking spacer at ease. It would be nice to have someone to chat with during the voyage, but he'd soon grow weary of Devine if he remained a nervous wreck.

"Sir, I recognize you. You're Commander Tad Thatcher, aren't you?"

Thatcher narrowed his eyes slightly. *Now, how does he know that?* He'd always prided himself on being the best spacer he could be, but he hadn't risen high enough yet to acquire much of a reputation throughout the Fleet. "Yes," he said, slowly.

"We're going to the same place, sir. Uh, Tad, sir. That is—I'll be serving on the *New Jersey*. Frontier hired me, too. They told me it was you commanding her. I'll be in Engineering."

Thatcher suppressed a frown, as well as a faint tinge of regret. He'd been happy enough to befriend Devine for the purposes of camaraderie during their time on the freighter, but he preferred not to get overly comfortable with men and women who would be under his command. It was something his grandfather had taught him: "It might seem cold, Tad, but a captain who befriends his crew will hesitate to order them into battle. No one wants to put their friends in danger. And even a second's hesitation at a crucial moment can mean disaster for that same crew. If you truly want to care for them, and keep them safe, then you'll keep your distance."

But there was nothing for it now. He wasn't about to take back his invitation to have a drink with the lad. He'd just have to make sure the boundaries between captain and crewmember were clear once they boarded the *New Jersey*.

"That's wonderful. Jimmy. Now, let's go have that drink."

Under the warm lights of the freighter's wood-paneled taproom, one drink turned into two, though Thatcher politely stated that the second would be his last. Even so, it apparently didn't take very much alcohol to loosen Devine's tongue about all manner of topics.

"The U.S. should never have let the UNC limit our Fleet," he was opining at the moment. "Everyone must see that now, with the Xanthic breathing down our necks. Every nation should have been building up their fleets since we took to space, so that we could all fight the bugs together."

"What about the Yidu Incident?" Thatcher asked.

Devine's scowl faltered, and he took another sip of beer as he mulled the question over. "That was the Chinese," he said at last. "Sure, maybe *their* fleet should have been limited. But why ours?"

"They never would have agreed to it, otherwise. There could have been war. And that would have been even worse."

In truth, Thatcher also had his reservations about the control the United Nations and Colonies exercised over the world's space fleets, and he certainly had them about the UNC itself. But the restrictions *had* resulted in peace among the nations, even before the Xanthic's first attack. Peace in space, at least. And the horror of space warfare was something the public had cried out against loudly, in unison. Once it had gotten its first taste.

Twenty years before the discovery of the Dawn Cluster, and thirty years after the Colony of Yidu's establishment, the colonists there attempted to win their independence from the Motherland, thinking themselves protected by the vast expanse of space. They wanted to begin their own experiment with democracy, just as America had hundreds of years before.

Yidu's experiment was short-lived. A Chinese destroyer was soon sent to the colony from Earth, a journey involving three separate jump gates. Once it arrived, it expended its arsenal of warheads, turning the colony to ash. It was assumed that no one survived—no structures were left standing, and Yidu's harsh, wintry climate surely claimed anyone who managed to escape the city in time.

The ensuing outcry was swift, as well as the backlash. Country after country imposed harsh sanctions against China, led by the U.S. For its part, Shanghai tried to claim that the destroyer had been taken over by patriotic mutineers, who'd nuked the colony on their own, without government approval. Thatcher had never met anyone who bought that line. Not even his own wife, who was Chinese.

War loomed, and the public panicked. At that time, humanity had fewer than a hundred spacefaring warships to its name, but the example of Yidu had shown what those ships could do to the Earth, as well as any colony a hostile nation might turn its attention toward.

In the end, an international compromise had saved humanity. The UNC, having only recently added the "C" to its name, for "Colonies," proposed a limit on every nation's space fleet, proportionate to its GDP—and proportionate to the dues it was able to pay the UNC, of course. Going forward, every warship would also be tracked by the UNC, who would destroy any vessel that showed the first sign of mutiny.

The plan had had its opponents. But the public was scared, and they turned out in the thousands, then the millions, to pressure their governments to give in. And give in they did. To prevent another Yidu, the UNC would maintain strict control of any technology that might facilitate the waging of war in space. To do that would require a system of widespread, automated surveillance, to alert the UNC overseers the moment anyone began to pursue the development of such a technology. In that instance, the budding technologist would be offered a job, and if they refused, then they would be threatened with a prison sentence unless they ceased their activities.

And so the UNC accrued all the newest technology to itself. With its technological trove, it built itself a super-fleet, so that it could enforce its new role as interstellar policeman.

What's better? Thatcher asked himself. *Armageddon, or what we have now?*

He knew the answer, of course. He vastly preferred the world where humanity survived—a world that had Lin in it, and their unborn son.

But he hated the corruption, and he hated the favoritism. A U.S. captain hadn't been chosen to command a UNC super-ship for almost a decade, now. The U.S. was still filled with freedom-loving citizens, even if few of them remembered a time when true freedom existed. For that, they were punished. Ironically, China was favored, probably because their society fit the UNC's model of governance so well.

I just hope the UNC's fleet will be enough to hold back the Xanthic. If not, we gave up our freedoms for nothing.

CHAPTER FIVE

Aboard the *Goliath*
Underway to Unity System, Earth Local Space
Earth Year 2290

THATCHER SAT IN THE ANGULAR DESK CHAIR PROVIDED HIM, NEXT to his cabin's bunk, immersed in the Fleet textbooks he'd downloaded to his Lenses. He could have laid down on the bed in better comfort to read, but he knew from experience that if he did that he would soon be fast asleep.

Rear Admiral Faulkner had predicted Thatcher would barely need to study for the exams Frontier Security used to gauge fitness for command, but as a rule, Thatcher preferred to leave nothing to chance. Not if he could all but guarantee success by spending the time to prepare.

The wormhole to the Dawn Cluster lay several systems away from Sol, and it would take the better part of six days to make the journey. After his drinks with Ensign Devine, Thatcher retired to his cabin, nestled his duffel bag between the bunk and the wall, and dragged the chair out from the bolted-down desk. With that, he started in.

As he reviewed the list of exams he would need to challenge by the time the *Goliath* reached Lincoln Station in Sunrise, the system on the other side of the wormhole, he raised an eyebrow at how little time would be devoted to testing his knowledge of tactics. There was plenty of focus on the technology that would be at his disposal—namely, the ship. Proper shiphandling, the *New Jersey*'s antimatter reactor-based engineering complex, and yes, the state-of-the-art Gladius combat system, including the Ogre and Hellborn missiles it was capable of firing, the railgun turrets, and the primary and secondary laser batteries. The Gladius system was designed to be modular, which meant that, at a well-appointed station, a captain could adapt his complement of weapons to a coming engagement with relative ease.

There was plenty of material on the damage the *New Jersey* was capable of dealing, but Frontier seemed much more concerned about his ability to manage the crew and keep them safe than about his prowess in battle. "Conflict De-escalation" got an entire exam unto itself, and so did making sure Thatcher wouldn't run afoul of Interstellar Law, which could expose the company to legal action.

It was all vital, he had to admit. He'd much rather talk than fight, if it could be avoided. Any sane captain would choose that over exposing his crew to unnecessary danger. But combat tended to find warships sooner or later, and it worried him that Frontier was apparently so confident in its tech that they devoted this little thought to using that tech to defeat adversaries.

Until now, that approach had probably served them, dealing with single pirate ships out in the Contested Systems. But with the pirates banding together, and war with the Xanthic looming, Thatcher just hoped the Cluster's other PMCs didn't share Frontier's blind spot. If so, they'd have to step up their game considerably, and quickly.

After four days of cramming—luckily, he truly had known most of the material, from years of serving on various Fleet commands—he fished his keyboard out of his luggage, unfolded it atop the desk, and initiated his first exam. O'Malley had transmitted the program that administered the exams to his Lenses before he'd left Norfolk. Now, it started a two-hour timer in the upper-right corner of his field of vision, and it blocked his access to every other Lens function until either the timer ran out or he submitted the completed exam. If he removed his Lenses, the software would detect it, and automatically fail him. This was all designed to prevent cheating.

He spent the entire fifth day writing exam after exam, taking only short breaks to use the head or eat. At 0800 on the sixth day, the captain came on the PA:

"Passengers and crew of the *Goliath*, this is Captain Therese Martoglio, informing you that we've just arrived in the Unity System. It will take us just over eleven hours to reach the system's Aphesis Band, where the wormhole is located. After that, another five hours will take us to Lincoln Station, expected arrival 0100. Passengers, you are asked to be ready to disembark at that time, as the *Goliath* will need to proceed promptly to the next destination to stay on schedule. Thank you for traveling with us, and I hope your last day aboard is a pleasant one."

The Unity System. Where all nations and peoples enjoyed equal access to the wormhole, overseen by the UNC. There was also a Unity Region in the Dawn Cluster—Thatcher would pass through it on his way to Planet Oasis. Here, the wormhole orbited Unity on its outskirts, nestled inside a plasma field called the Aphesis Band.

Humanity had been transiting back and forth through the wormhole for a century. In recent decades, it had even been deemed safe enough for colonists. Even so, Thatcher felt a knot of anxiety at the base of his throat. It had been there for a couple of days, and it was getting worse the closer they got to the great gateway.

He'd never visited the Dawn Cluster before. He'd read about

the first ships to go through, whose crews had almost all been claimed by cancer a few years later, after being bathed in radiation by the wormhole. Their onboard Geiger counters had told the tale, but by then it was far too late.

After that, the UNC had banned all wormhole travel while it took a year to develop the hull shielding necessary to protect crews. Yet another technology it hoarded to itself, though it outfitted any ship that wanted the shielding, setting its own price for the upgrade.

Thatcher knew he had nothing to fear from the transition through the wormhole—these days, any ship that went to the Cluster carried the shielding necessary to protect her occupants. But the idea of traveling tens of thousands of light years in an instant boggled his mind, and his anxiety spiked whenever he considered how far from Lin it would put him.

But that was far from the only source of his anxiety. At least half of it stemmed from the fact that he was mere hours away from boarding his first command—his childhood dream, realized years ahead of schedule. Was he truly ready? Or would he make some fatal error, when the responsibility for his ship and crew lay squarely on his shoulders?

He wrote the last exam, checked over his answers, and submitted it a half hour before the timer ran out. With that, he sat in the rigid chair and stared at the bulkhead, forcing himself to breathe deeply. But the knot of tension remained.

To distract himself, he called up a news site, whose main headline did nothing to calm him:

"STRANGE UNDERGROUND GROWTHS SUSPECTED TO BE XANTHIC INCUBATION PODS."

Stiffening, he read the story twice, his eyes lingering on the featured images. The jaundiced pods had been found on Earth, in caves below the city of Trieste, in Italy. Sinewy tendrils connected the pregnant-looking sacks to the floor and ceiling of the caves. In the first image, men with flamethrowers were turning the pods to ash.

But Barton was crawling with Xanthic. If the pods are under Italy, they're probably everywhere else, too.

I have to go back.

Except, he wasn't clear on how he would do that. He doubted the freighter would turn around just to deliver him back to Earth orbit, and he couldn't afford to hire another vessel to bring him back. Possibly, he could pay a shuttle pilot to divert course and dock with the *Goliath* to pick him up, then to take him to another freighter bound for Earth. But it would put a significant dent in his and Lin's savings. How would she take it if he reacted that way? If he managed to screw up his job with Frontier right after leaving the Fleet?

The last paragraph of the news story mentioned that planet-wide evacuations were already underway, as authorities scoured the planet for more pods. There was nothing he would accomplish by returning to Earth that the UNC and the U.S. military wouldn't accomplish anyway. So he set about first messaging Rear Admiral Faulkner, asking that Lin and her parents be given priority in the queue for evacuation, along with his own parents. That done, he messaged Lin, urging her to get off Earth as soon as possible and go to one of the Lunar Colonies. He reasoned that the Xanthic pods probably wouldn't survive on the moon, without any atmosphere. She'd be safe there. As safe as it was possible to be in Earth Local Space, right now.

His messages sent, he leaned against the chair's hard back, chewing the inside of his cheek and wondering if he was doing the right thing. In his heart, he knew that Admiral Faulkner was right: he'd be making the biggest difference exactly where he was going.

But Lin's face filled his mind's eye, and he couldn't help feeling as though he was leaving her and their unborn son to the aliens.

CHAPTER SIX

Lincoln Station
Sunrise System, Clime Region
Earth Year 2290

"So I was right," Thatcher muttered to himself as he marched down the long access tube leading to the *New Jersey*. "There will be no change of command ceremony."

Upon disembarking from the *Goliath*, he'd received nothing more than directions to the open-space docking bay where the *New Jersey* awaited him, and orders to proceed to Oasis Colony after taking command. There had been nothing in the message he'd received about a time at which the crew would be mustered and the national anthem played—a time at which he would officially assume command. Neither had there been any indication of his performance on the exams he'd challenged, though he had to assume he'd at least passed them.

"The *New Jersey*," he said, emphasizing the ship's title sardonically. He was beginning to suspect that Frontier's habit of naming its starships after U.S. Navy ships of old was nothing more than a marketing gimmick, to give the impression that the company's ships conducted themselves just like U.S. Space Fleet ships.

The Admiral seemed to buy that line. Now I get to find out if it holds up.

In truth, he'd worried about this ever since hearing the *New Jersey* was a light cruiser. The original *New Jersey* had been a battleship, and it hadn't carried any missiles at all. Minor details to some, but in Thatcher's mind they loomed large.

This wasn't how he'd expected to feel the day he assumed his first command. Lincoln Station itself had contributed to his irritation, with its winding ways, nearly unnavigable even with the directions he'd been given. To a newcomer, it was a bewildering warren of identical corridors, hatches, and bays. The American government owned the sprawling station, and it was one of many superstructures littered throughout the Sunrise System, all owned by various countries. Any nation that could afford a station here was permitted only one, and so those owned by governments with sufficiently high GDPs tended to grow over time, most becoming confounding tangles.

These stations' safety was virtually guaranteed, with the presence of so many UNC super-ships—massive fighter drone carriers and dreadnoughts that bristled weaponry, both which dwarfed everything else in the system. Sunrise was considered a "cold" system, along with the rest of Clime Region, with the chance of conflict breaking out here very close to zero. The four neighboring regions were also cold, and beyond them were the warm regions—where Oasis was located. The Contested Regions beyond those were termed "hot."

Thatcher reached the part of the access tube where the upper half became transparent, and his eyes fell on the *New Jersey* herself.

"My God," he said, drawing up short to behold the sleek craft. "She's beautiful."

All thoughts of Frontier Security's seeming impropriety

vanished as he let his eyes feast on the waiting starship. The yard workers had done a stellar job of replacing the hull sections damaged when the *New Jersey* fled the ambush that had awaited her in the first system of the Olent Region. Thatcher had winced his way through the report from that engagement: if there hadn't been an accompanying electronic warfare ship to unleash an omnidirectional jamming burst and cover their escape, the pirates or the Xanthic likely would have gotten both ships.

But now, he couldn't find any evidence of the beating she'd taken after her shields went down, not anywhere along her gleaming, five hundred meter length. The chunky railgun accelerator for flinging warhead-tipped missiles at high speeds, the primary laser focusing array, the automated turrets, the broad hull—all six hundred thousand tons looked new and burnished to a satisfying sheen.

He found himself drawing deep breaths, fighting to steady himself. This was what he'd spent years working toward. The reason he'd tried to lead the perfect career, with impeccable service, impeccable decorum. So what if Frontier wasn't the U.S. Space Fleet analog it presented itself as? He would make it work.

The marine sentry standing at ease outside the cruiser's personnel hatch came to attention as Thatcher approached, sketching a passable salute. "Welcome to the *New Jersey*, Captain Thatcher," he said.

Thatcher regarded him coldly, saying nothing. By Fleet custom, it wasn't appropriate to acknowledge him as captain until he'd assumed command. Surely this marine should know that—he must have served with the actual U.S. marines at some point.

Either way, he wilted under Thatcher's glare, then turned to key open the hatch to admit him.

"Aren't you going to inspect my ID?" Thatcher asked before stepping onto the *New Jersey*.

"Why, sir, we all know who you—"

"I don't much care who you *think* I am, Sergeant. Every person approaching this ship is to be properly IDed."

They looked at each other for a protracted moment, the baffled sergeant apparently at a loss. Finally, he held out his hand and said, "May I see your ID, sir?"

Thatcher slapped the card into the man's hand and continued to study the marine as he made a show of comparing the holographic image there to his new captain's face. After a few seconds, he returned the card with a salute. Nodding curtly, Thatcher proceeded into the *Jersey*.

He rounded the first bend into an empty passageway. Would the marine know enough to alert the ship's XO to Thatcher's presence, or would he be forced to wander his new command like a lost tourist until he found the CIC?

The next passageway was similarly empty, and he took the opportunity to run his index finger along the bulkhead. It came back dark with grime, and he frowned at it ferociously.

The next corner gave way to reveal his green-eyed Executive Officer at last, walking briskly toward him. They both came up short to avoid a collision, and the XO stepped back, saluting smartly.

Thatcher returned it. "Permission to come aboard?" he ground out, even though he was clearly already on board, since Lieutenant Commander Billy Candle had failed to greet him at the personnel hatch.

"Permission granted," Candle said. If his own indecorum made him uneasy, it didn't show. "May I escort you to the CIC, sir?"

"Thank you, Commander." So they *were* flirting with Fleet protocol, then. Well, two could play at that game. Custom said Thatcher should wait until officially assuming command before asserting his will, but as they walked together he said, "The state of these passageways is unacceptable. Have Cleaning Stations not been implemented?"

Candle cleared his throat. "The crew has had...other priorities of late, sir."

"Unless we are actively engaging enemy ships, maintaining a clean and orderly ship must be our *first* priority, Commander. Are we currently engaging an enemy ship?"

"Um, no, sir. Not at present."

"Then it will be your first task to assign Cleaning Stations if they have not already been assigned, and then to tour the ship with the Command Master Chief between 0800 and 0900 to ensure every crewmember is doing his or her part. Is that clear?"

"Aye, sir."

"Good."

Thatcher admired Candle's ability to conceal his resentment toward the changes his new master's arrival clearly represented. But there was no doubt the resentment was there—Thatcher had spent far too many years observing his subordinates to miss it.

This XO is capable of frightful deceit, if he turns his mind to it. I'm sure of it.

Most seasoned captains would avoid making radical changes from the way his predecessor had run things—certainly on the first day of command. But from what Thatcher had already seen, he sensed that implementing great change was unavoidable.

He intended to preside over a proper warship, not a filthy, disorderly tub.

CHAPTER SEVEN

Aboard the *New Jersey*
Sparkling Vista System, Clime Region
Earth Year 2290

"YOU THERE," THE STOCKY COMMAND MASTER CHIEF BARKED AT a pair of seamen chatting over their mop handles. "Get back to work, you, and don't have me repeat myself." Stan Wainman turned to his captain with a self-satisfied grin as the seamen resumed their mopping with vigor, and Thatcher offered a grave nod. They and Lieutenant Commander Candle continued along the passageway, observing the crew at their Cleaning Stations.

Thatcher liked Wainman. He seemed like a man who'd been utterly henpecked by the crew under his last captain. That made sense, as Captain Vaughn had apparently given his subordinates most everything they wanted, including a steady stream of prize money. As far as Thatcher could tell, Wainman found his more authoritarian approach to be a breath of fresh air.

Of course, his "approach" wouldn't have been considered particularly authoritarian in the real Fleet. Indeed, he almost certainly wouldn't have had to make most of these changes, since they would have been part of the normal running of a Fleet starship.

This was the first time in a week he'd joined Candle and Wainman in their oversight of Cleaning Stations. For the first week of his command, he'd walked with them every day, to help the crew understand exactly how serious he was about maintaining order aboard the *New Jersey*. He'd also filled his early days with mess deck and uniform inspections, and spot checks—an unusual number of them for the commanding officer to perform. But until he could be sure his officers and chief petty officers had gotten into the habit of performing them routinely, he would continue to hammer home the message himself: the *New Jersey* was no filthy space tub, but a proper warship, properly maintained.

It was good to have an ally in his efforts—and not one who just went through the motions, like Candle, but a true enthusiast like Wainman. The command master chief had also brought some startling rumors to his attention, of fraternization between the ship's officers and enlisted men. Wainman had also "heard" of seamen and petty officers getting invited into officer's country, to fill out poker games or simply to get drunk and gossip.

It was plain to Thatcher that these were more than rumors, and that Wainman knew exactly what was going on between the *New Jersey*'s officers and crew. But it was well that he'd characterized the news as "rumors," since actual evidence would have forced Thatcher to start discharging crewmembers.

It was much better to make a brief announcement over the 1MC: "This is Captain Thatcher. All crew are reminded that interaction between enlisted crewmembers and ship's officers is to be limited to official communication only. Fraternization between a unit's officers and enlisted members is strongly discouraged, and inappropriate relationships will result in discharge."

He didn't dare try taking their alcohol away—not yet,

anyway. But U.S. Space Fleet ships were dry, and the *New Jersey* would be too. Eventually.

One thing about Candle, he's certainly efficient. The XO had ensured the *New Jersey* was ready to get underway the moment her captain arrived, and since then they'd been making good time through the Clime Region. Soon, they would pass through the regional jump gate, into Unity Region, and then into Dupliss, where most American colonies were. Including Oasis Colony.

The three men entered the engineering plant, where Ensign Jimmy Devine was busy scrubbing a check valve with a sopping sponge. When he saw the officers enter, he dropped the sponge and came to attention, snapping off a salute.

"At ease, Ensign," Thatcher murmured, and Devine took up his sponge again with just as much verve as before.

Thatcher caught himself frowning as he remembered his first day of command, when the lad had greeted him in an overly familiar way.

"Your boots could use some work, Devine," Thatcher had snapped in response, and the ensign had reddened from collar to cap.

"Yes, sir," he'd choked out.

A few other engineers had been within earshot. Under normal circumstances, Thatcher wouldn't have reacted with quite so much force, but given the stance he'd taken against fraternization he couldn't very well tolerate it in himself. They weren't aboard the *Goliath* any longer.

The hour of Cleaning Stations came to an end, and they completed their tour about the *New Jersey*. "Candle, I want you to meet me in my office at 1000. Bring the chief engineer's report on his inspection of the Hellborns' onboard computers with you."

"Aye, sir."

Thatcher nodded, then continued down the passageway toward his office. The new Hellborns were Frontier's answer to the Ogre-class missiles getting hacked by the Xanthic in Olent. This version was supposed to be unhackable, but Thatcher knew no such thing existed. There was only the arms race between security experts and attackers—a balance of back doors and exploits.

He could sense the crew's unease as he passed them by, their eyes sliding off him as they came to attention and saluted. "At ease," he muttered, again and again. "At ease." The words seemed to take on a second meaning.

These men and women had no doubt joined the private military sector to make money and to escape the Fleet's stringent protocols. Now, here was a captain who enforced them more strongly than anyone they were likely to have served under in the Fleet.

But Thatcher was a traditionalist. He didn't believe in the modern freewheeling way of doing things—the way that preserved feelings wherever it could, treating its subjects with kid gloves.

Rather, he believed there were only a few ways to run an effective ship, and they'd all been discovered already. He didn't command a social science experiment, but a military vessel. The crew would simply have to get used to it.

CHAPTER EIGHT

New Houston, Oasis Colony
Freedom System, Dupliss Region
Earth Year 2290

"Welcome to Oasis, Commander." As they shook, Veronica Rose's hand was soft but firm against his. "I trust your voyage from the wormhole was an uneventful one."

Thatcher nodded. "Everyone's always on their best behavior, under the watchful eye of the UNC."

The CEO of Frontier Security chuckled softly. "If only that eye cast its gaze on the Contested Systems, from time to time." The CEO gave off a subtle lilac scent he found soothing.

His efforts to focus on her face were thwarted by the magnificence of the view through her floor-to-ceiling window. Lush, rolling hills and thick vegetation made it hard to believe he was looking at a densely populated city. A strong wind rustled the leafy canopy, revealing patches of asphalt far below, and here and there buildings poked above the tall forest ceiling.

"The trees here grow unusually tall," he remarked.

"So they do. Oasis is well-named. Won't you take a seat?"

Her tanned arm stretched toward a chair opposite hers, and he sank into it, reluctant to relinquish the stunning view.

Rose took her own seat and met his eyes with the frank directness that came with power. Her gleaming, raven hair flowed down to her shoulders, perfectly straight—a marked contrast with her pale visage. "It's a great privilege to count you among Frontier's ranks, Commander. I can hardly believe our luck. Few prospective captains come as highly recommended as you did, and I believe your talents were being wasted while you waited for your own command in the Fleet."

He felt himself stiffen slightly at her suggestion the Fleet was doing anything except its best, given the conditions the UNC imposed on it. But he remained silent.

Rose tilted her head. "I understand you were reluctant to leave the Fleet."

"Yes." He saw no point in masking his feelings.

"I know there's a lot of cynicism in Earth Local Space about whether Cluster corps actually care about human prosperity— whether all that talk is just marketing. I want you to know that my company *does* care. We care about the Americans living on Oasis. We care that we're an American company, serving the US government. And we care about spreading American values."

Spreading those values is easier said than done, with everyone under the UNC's thumb. But again, he reserved comment.

"I'm especially excited by the tactical prowess you demonstrated in the Command Leadership exams you challenged while en route to the Dawn Cluster. You performed well in all the exams, but tactics was where you truly shined. And that's what we need out here."

"Very good," he said, a little tersely. He sensed that he was being buttered up for something, and he felt impatient to know what it was.

"There is one little issue, however." The CEO folded her

slender fingers in front of her trim stomach, and he knew the time had arrived. "I've been receiving reports that certain members of your crew feel…disquieted about changes you've made aboard the *New Jersey*. And in my experience, for every person that speaks out, ten more share the same concern."

"What changes, exactly?"

"Your predecessor, Captain Vaughn, was very accommo- dating when it came to his crew. They're used to a commander who listens to their concerns, and makes provisions for—"

"I fully intend to listen to the concerns of my crew, Ms. Rose. Any good starship captain does that. I've already engaged several of the crew individually about their sense of the *New Jersey*, as well as their own personal hopes and fears, their mood, their family lives or lack thereof. I also appear to have an excellent command master chief to relay crew concerns to me. But if I can be candid, ma'am, a lack of crew comfort is not the main issue aboard the *Jersey*. It's too *much* crew comfort."

She visibly drew breath, her slender shoulders rising and fall- ing. "Commander, the rigid standards that apply in the Fleet simply don't apply on Frontier ships. Trying to recreate the envi- ronment you experienced there won't fly aboard one of our vessels."

He continued to meet the CEO's gaze, keeping his expression neutral. "I am here because a superior suggested to me that securing the Dawn Cluster is strategically important, both for America and for humanity. I was told that serving on a Frontier starship would be nearly indistinguishable from a properly run USSF ship. If that isn't the case, and you would prefer to let me go, I would be more than happy to return to Earth and reenlist in the Fleet. But I *can* get the job done for you, ma'am. I can best the pirates who presume to gather in force against American ships. I can get to the bottom of the Xanthic's presence here. But only if I'm allowed to run my ship as I see fit."

Veronica Rose studied him for a long time, one eyebrow

arched far above the other. Then, the errant brow relaxed, and she chuckled. "You are a formidable man, aren't you Tad Thatcher? I shouldn't have expected anything less than this from you, I suppose."

He remained silent.

"Letting you go is the last thing I want to do. I'm not afraid to confess that we need you, Commander. So you *will* have your way with this—I just hope your knowledge of tactics is matched by your ability to control a crew."

"Are you worried about a mutiny?" Thatcher asked, eyes narrowed.

"It's always a possibility, in the deep, dark of space. But the more likely outcome is that your crew will simply seek positions with other companies once their contracts run out. Employee attrition is a big problem, here in the Cluster. It's a race to the bottom between private military companies, to see who can best compromise their effectiveness in order to cater to their workers. As you've already gathered, Captain Vaughn was extremely popular with the Frontier employees that served under him. So far, you are not. But as I said, I need you, and so it will be up to you to figure out a way to make sure your crew doesn't abandon ship at the earliest opportunity."

A silence descended upon them, and Thatcher's gaze wandered out to the bright blue sky beyond Rose, visible through the segmented glass. Planetside sights always riveted his attention like this, even on Earth. They had become a novelty in his life, which was so much spent aboard the cold metal of starships, adrift in the void of space.

"There's another matter, Commander," Rose said, snapping the silence in two. "You no doubt noticed the warships distributed throughout the Freedom System, guarding America's primary colony in the Cluster."

He nodded. "They belong to Reardon Interstellar, do they not?" That both companies had been given a contract by the government to defend Oasis was no secret to anyone interested in knowing.

"They do. That much is public knowledge, but there's much that goes on in the Dawn Cluster that isn't. How would you react if I told you that a significant amount of the violence that occurs on the Cluster's periphery isn't between corporation and pirate, but corporation and corporation?"

The question made him blink. "But the UNC prohibits fighting."

"Yes, but they don't have the super-ships to patrol the whole Cluster, do they Commander? The attackers always do their best to seem like pirates—that's easiest if they manage to destroy their prey. There are also rumors of corps simply paying pirates to execute such attacks."

"For what purpose?"

"The usual one. If the victim corporation considers a system too hot to do business in, it will withdraw to safer, less profitable stars. And it's never long before the shadow aggressor moves into the system where the attacks occurred. Generally, they're smart enough to ensure there's a lack of concrete evidence—if pressed, they'll say they must simply have a higher risk-tolerance than the corp that fled. But everyone knows what really went on."

"Does Reardon Interstellar have a history of being involved in such situations?"

"It does indeed. Not only that, I'm certain they have an arrangement with some pirates in the north. Why else would they grow so bold as to band together and attack our vessels directly? Reardon's been tasked with protecting the Freedom System, whereas Frontier is responsible for patrolling the surrounding systems and regions, scanning for threats and answering them before they become unmanageable. But Reardon wants *both* contracts, and they're in the perfect position to make that happen, sitting pretty inside this system while their pirate lackeys pick us apart."

Thatcher felt the corner of his mouth twitch—a tick that often befell him as he was sizing up a problem. "Do you think Reardon would stoop so low as to work with the Xanthic?"

"Honestly, Commander, it wouldn't surprise me."

"I see. Would it be possible for a logistics ship to also be deployed with the *New Jersey*?"

"I'm afraid not. You may have noticed the *Squall* maintaining orbit over Oasis—the same electronic warfare ship that enabled your cruiser to escape her last encounter with pirates and Xanthic. You will have her, but there is nothing else available for you to take. I am sorry. All other Frontier ships are busy carrying out patrols and assignments vital to the safety of this region. As I said, Commander, I need you. But really, I was understating it. What I *really* need is for you to perform a miracle."

CHAPTER NINE

Aboard the *New Jersey*
Ramage System, Dupliss Region
Earth Year 2290

EVERY ENGAGEMENT IS A PUZZLE YOU MUST SOLVE IN MINUTES.
His grandfather had been fond of saying that. Yes, Edward
Thatcher would concede, space engagements unfolded over
hours, not minutes. But those hours had to be spent executing the
plan you devised upon first spotting the enemy. Switching tacks
halfway through a battle *could* work, but more often it ended in
ruin.

As the *New Jersey* moved from jump zone to jump gate,
sailing through the final warm systems before transitioning into
hot ones, Thatcher tried to fit together as many of the puzzle's
pieces as he could in advance.

He'd requested information on the *New Jersey*'s capabilities
from the chief engineer, at a level of detail that drew a blank
stare from the rotund Scottish man. Apparently Frontier captains
didn't take that deep an interest in what their ships could do. *She*

can move and she can fire her guns. That's enough for most, I suppose.

Sitting at his desk inside his cramped office, which made economical use of space—very economical—he looked up. It had suddenly occurred to him to wonder how a man as fat as Ainsley, the chief engineer, managed to fit into the engineering plant's various nooks and crannies. How *did* the man do his job?

"He must be a champion delegator," Thatcher murmured. Then he returned to his study of the specifications listed on the holographic screen, which extended from his desk and would retract again at the tap of a button.

In particular, his eyes scanned the information detailing the new Hellborn missile's acceleration profile. According to what he was seeing, the missile attained its top speed quickly, but its acceleration then leveled off in order to conserve enough fuel to reach the target, and track it if necessary.

The *New Jersey*, on the other hand, could afford to continue accelerating throughout an entire engagement. Which meant that, provided a Hellborn was loosed early enough, there was nothing to stop her from catching up to her own missile.

"Interesting," he muttered. It was something an old sea-bound Navy ship could never have done. But during his time in the Fleet, he'd become convinced that most captains still conceived of their ships in naval terms and thought of space engagements as sea battles that simply happened in the uncaring void.

And why not? Because of the Yidu incident, humanity had barely experienced space warfare. Yes, they'd fought back the Xanthic fleets, but any serious analyst admitted that outcome had been due to having greater numbers. The Xanthic engagements had taught Earth's space fleets a few things, but not enough, in Thatcher's view. There was still a lot of room for innovation. For trying things no one had thought of, and shaping the face of warfare for centuries to come.

The hatch buzzed, and Thatcher swiped his screen clear before tapping the button to retract it, and then the one to activate the com. "Yes?"

"It's Major Hancock, if you please, sir. Might I speak with you?"

"Come in." Thatcher tapped the button to admit his marine commander.

The hatch swung inward, and the swarthy Englishman swaggered in, his muscled arms held out to both sides as they strained the fabric of his brown service uniform. Hancock closed the hatch behind him and then came to attention, eyeing the narrow chair in front of the desk all the while.

"At ease," Thatcher said. "Take a seat."

"Sorry to bother you, sir. I won't waste your time with chitchat. It's just that…well, there's something I think you ought to know."

Thatcher raised both eyebrows and waited for Hancock to spit it out.

"Sir, as I'm sure you know, the crew on this rig is used to prize money, and lots of it. Captain Vaughn kept them bathing in it, but now there's talk on the mess decks that they won't see a fraction of what they used to, going forward. With that, on top of the rules and such you've imposed, there are a lot of discontented spacers on this ship."

None of this was news to Thatcher. He was capable of reading his own crew, and it didn't take very long aboard warships to figure out that spacers didn't like change. Either way, he'd made a habit of calling Ensign Jimmy Devine to his office regularly, under the guise of reprimanding him for this and that. His fellow engineers thought that Thatcher had a particular dislike for Devine, but in truth the lad was feeding him information about the gossip he heard while working in the engineering plant and dining in the mess. Thatcher told Devine that his performance report would be glowing so long as his comportment remained exemplary. That assurance had pleased Devine to no end, and he'd answered with a hearty "Yes, sir" before returning to his duties.

Still, Hancock's presence means something. Maybe it's something I can use. "Are you here to complain on the crew's behalf, then, Major?"

"Huh? Oh, heavens no, Captain! I'm here to make sure you know that no matter how surly the crew gets, order *will* be maintained aboard this ship. I intend to see to that personally."

That's good, considering it's your job. "You're not concerned about a reduction in prize money, then."

"That's just it, sir. Old Captain Vaughn never cut my marines in on any prize money, because he always managed to secure pirate ships' surrender without our help. He went out of his way to do that, and it's not hard to see why. Splitting it with us would mean spreading it thinner, see? And so it don't bother me none if there's less prize money. Especially if you intend to divide up any prize money we *do* win more fairly than Captain Vaughn did."

Thatcher stared at Hancock, fighting hard to mask his sudden contempt for the man. So he'd come here to try and bargain with his commanding officer, using the execution of his duty as a bargaining chip, had he?

He deserves a sharp rebuke, at the very least. But Thatcher knew better than to deliver that just yet. No matter the man's motivations, Hancock had just revealed himself as one of the few allies Thatcher had aboard the *New Jersey.*

I need to determine which has greater sway over his marines' hearts—their loyalty to him or their sense of duty. Until I do, I need this man.

"Thank you, Major. I appreciate your assurance. It brings me great peace of mind."

"I knew it would, sir," Hancock said, a grin spreading across his face like an oil slick over water.

"Dismissed."

The major rose to his feet, saluted, and left Thatcher with his thoughts.

The Jersey's *about to head into battle without proper support. No logistics ship to bolster her shields, and only her own repair drones to keep her hull intact.*

On top of that, he was sitting on a discontented crew—a serious blow to any vessel's combat effectiveness.

By any measure, things looked bleak indeed for the light armored cruiser. Nevertheless, he grew a smile of his own.

I'll simply have to show our enemies something they've never seen before.

CHAPTER TEN

Aboard the *New Jersey*
Elsin System, Tempore Region
Earth Year 2290

"I'VE DEVISED A PLAN FOR DEFEATING THE PIRATE BATTLE GROUP
that bested the *New Jersey* before," Thatcher said, meeting the
gaze of each of his department heads in turn. They peered at him
from their spots around the ship's conference room, which was
situated near the CIC. "I think it'll even give the Xanthic warship
a run for its money. Either way, I don't intend to share that plan
with anyone aboard this ship."

The department heads—his chief tactical officer, chief engineer, operations officer, senior supply officer, as well as his XO
—all looked at him with expressions ranging from confused to
aghast. Tim Ortega, his chief tactical officer, opened his mouth
for a protracted second, then closed it.

"During my first weeks aboard the *New Jersey*, I've come to
the conclusion that the environment here is an abysmal one for
maintaining proper OPSEC. As you know, I come from the U.S.
Space Fleet, where it can generally be expected that the reason

spacers are serving in the first place is out of loyalty to their country—to the cause of keeping her safe, and of defending what freedoms she has left. Certainly, no one joins up for the pay.

"But here on the *Jersey*, Frontier's employees are far more concerned with their own personal advancement than any cause we might devote her faculties to. That seems to be true despite the fact that stabilizing the Dawn Cluster will prove vital to humanity's victory over the Xanthic. Very well. I will work with what I have been given, and I will do it in the following manner: in the coming engagement, department heads are to be at the ready, to ensure any order I give is executed by subordinates swiftly and effectively. You will be held personally responsible for any failure on your subordinates' part, so I would advise you find a way to properly motivate them that doesn't involve appeals pertaining to prize money. Do not concern yourself with pondering any order you find odd or counterintuitive. Simply execute each order promptly, and all will be well."

His executive officer, Billy Candle, cleared his throat. "Captain—"

"Speaking of prize money," Thatcher said, elevating his volume to indicate that Candle should silence himself, "the *New Jersey*'s allotment of proceeds from any stolen goods we recover during the next month will be donated to the development of civil society on Planet Oasis. The same will occur in the following month, and then the next, and it will continue until I have become convinced that the crew's primary motivations have shifted to those of service and duty."

He leaned back in his seat, crossing his arms and allowing himself an abbreviated smirk as he took in their expressions, which this time were almost uniformly stunned. As he did, he reflected that Lin would welcome the influx of cash that any prize money would represent, especially considering the captain always received the largest share. That kind of money could afford her and their son more comfort, and it would certainly mean a better future for young Edward.

But none of that would matter if he allowed his ship to be destroyed because his crew was more motivated by greed than by working to ensure the *New Jersey* became the most effective weapon of war she could be.

Lin. He longed for her—longed for the familiar way her slender body fit into his as they slept. Longed for the freshness of her scent as she slipped between their sheets after her evening shower.

A message had caught up to him during his time on Oasis—two messages, actually. One from Rear Admiral Faulkner, which assured him that he would do everything in his power to keep Thatcher's family safe, and the other from Lin, letting him know that she and both their parents had arrived safely on Earth's moon.

And Edward. Our son.

They would be safe. The U.S. Space Fleet would fight to the last ship before allowing the Xanthic to get at Earth's civilians, and for all Thatcher's distrust of the UNC, he knew their super-ships would fight just as ardently.

They'll be safe. They have to be. If not, I'll have nothing left to fight for.

He knew that wasn't quite true. If they were to die, he would have one final thing to drive him—a path that had been followed by incensed warriors all throughout Earth's history. A burning impetus that could be boiled down to one bitter word.

Vengeance.

But he pushed that word out of his mind. It made him shudder, and it wouldn't do to even entertain the thought.

CHAPTER ELEVEN

Aboard the *New Jersey*
Gyve System, Olent Region
Earth Year 2290

"OPS, TELL THE *SQUALL* TO KEEP PACE WITH US. NAV, SEND OUR course to Lieutenant Guerrero for forwarding to the electronic warfare ship. And Lieutenant, I want the eWar ship to send directional jamming bursts at the enemy battle group the entire time it takes us to close."

"Aye, sir," came from the Nav and Ops stations. He liked how prompt and crisp their responses were—he could tell they were eager to prove to him that they weren't as money-motivated as he thought. Perhaps if they continued trying to prove that, it would eventually become true.

This time, the pirates had chosen a different system to lie in ambush—the Gyve System, which lay deeper inside Olent and had five jump gates connecting it to surrounding systems. So far, there was no sign of the Xanthic, but all seven pirate ships were clustered around a small planet orbiting Gyve on the system's outskirts. Thatcher assumed the rock had some importance for them, but even so, the pirates had given themselves five avenues of escape if things went poorly for them.

They did not expect things to go poorly, he knew. These were the same ships from before—to confirm that, it was barely necessary to compare the sensor data Lucy Guerrero had sent him to the video record of the engagement that had claimed Captain Vaughn's life. The last battle had borne every resemblance to a rout, and the pirates would have no reason to believe this one would end differently, even if their Xanthic friends weren't present. Thatcher was willing to bet that right now, their comms were alive with disbelieving laughter at the stupidity of Frontier's return.

It was exactly how he wanted them to feel, and a cursory study of the tactical display on his holoscreen offered further confirmation. The way their frontmost ships clustered together screamed sloppiness born of arrogance.

"Lieutenant Commander," Thatcher said with his eyes locked onto the back of his XO's head, his voice and face stern.

Candle turned, a slight jolt rocking him as he saw the expression on his captain's face. Throwing his XO off-balance at such a critical moment wouldn't have been his normal approach, but the *New Jersey* wasn't a normal command. He wanted his officers on their back feet, uncertain of themselves and anxious to justify their positions. Thatcher saw that as his best chance to extract a good performance from them.

"Fire the first Hellborn targeting the lead ship, the one in the center of the trio clustered at the enemy's fore."

Candle blinked. "Sir, with due respect, aren't we a bit far away to—"

"*Fire that missile,* XO."

"Aye, sir."

Thatcher had ordered a Hellborn loaded into the *Jersey*'s only missile tube the moment they'd left Planet Oasis, and so it took only seconds for the telltale shudder to announce the missile's departure.

"Missile away, Captain."

"Very good. Have the missile bay crew load the next, and make sure it's the one I specifically designated to be fired second." Thatcher twisted in his seat, toward the lanky man sitting at the Helm station. "Lieutenant Kitt, bring engines up to one hundred percent.

"Aye, Captain," Kitt answered softly, after a slight hesitation.

"We will continue to accelerate until we've caught up with our Hellborn. When we do, match our acceleration to the missile, and notify me at once."

"Aye, sir."

A heavy silence had fallen over the CIC, and Thatcher could almost hear his officers' thoughts. What was their captain doing, firing at the enemy from such a distance? And accelerating to *catch up* with their own missile?

That they'd never encountered a tactic like this was a dead certainty, because no one had. But Thatcher knew what he was doing.

He hoped.

"We've matched the missile's velocity, sir," Kitt said.

Thatcher nodded. "Fire the second Hellborn, XO. Target the same ship as before."

Shortly after they'd left the Dupliss Region, as they were sailing through Tempore, Thatcher had instructed his chief engineer to reprogram seven missiles so that they would communicate with any other Hellborns currently in play in order to match velocities with them.

He repeated the series of orders he'd given over the last several minutes—load one of the reprogrammed missiles, catch up to the Hellborns already fired, and loose the one in the tube. In this way, he built up an eight-missile barrage, where the *New*

Jersey was only supposed to be capable of launching one at a time.

The *Squall* continued its efforts to jam the enemy's sensors all the while. Thatcher figured Frontier was probably justified in its confidence that the new Hellborn model was resistant to hacking, but that didn't mean he intended to take any chances. The jamming should also serve to mask what was coming the pirates' way. Most captains waited until the last possible second to put up their shields, because of the massive power drain it involved. If these pirates failed to detect Thatcher's barrage, then they'd be sitting ducks.

The *New Jersey*'s railgun accelerator flung the eighth missile forward, and Thatcher gave his next orders. "Nav, set a new course that adjusts our attitude upward, enough that we'll steer well clear of any shrapnel."

"Aye, Captain," Lieutenant Sullivan replied in a thick Irish brogue.

"Ops, have the *Squall* stand by to execute an omnidirectional jamming burst five seconds before those missiles hit. She is to reverse course immediately after, return to the jump gate and head back to the previous system, to await us there for no more than twenty-four hours. If we don't arrive within that timeframe, she has my leave to return to Oasis." Thatcher eyed Candle. "XO, prepare to raise shields on my mark."

On Thatcher's holographic screen, he watched as the *New Jersey* and its deadly payload soared across the void toward the pirate formation. Raising his fingers to the display, he rotated the 3D image this way and that. This was nothing more than a needless compulsion. He knew his calculations were correct.

Nearly there...

"We just entered their lead ship's effective firing range, sir," said Lucy Guerrero.

"Steady," Thatcher said.

Candle's head twitched. "Sir—"

"I said steady."

"The lead three ships have fired missiles of their own, sir," Guerrero said. "Two each, for a total of six."

Candle was all but squirming at his station, now, as the missiles sped closer and he waited for his captain's command.

"Mark," Thatcher said.

With that, two things happened simultaneously. The *New Jersey*'s shields sprang to life, and the *Squall* executed its global jamming burst, washing out Thatcher's tactical display, which returned with a notice that the data displayed wasn't up-to-date.

They were flying blind, their attitude-adjusted trajectory bringing them just a couple thousand kilometers above the enemy formation. The CIC crew displayed their tension in various ways, some twitching, others sitting rigid at their stations, waiting for their displays to update.

"Two missiles just impacted our shields," Guerrero said. "Down to eighty-seven percent power."

Thatcher nodded. It would take more missiles than that to knock down the *Jersey*'s force field.

The sensor interference cleared at last, and tactical displays updated across the CIC, along with the main display shown inside the broad tank at the front. Two of the seven pirates ships had vanished from the battlespace. The *Squall* was well away, speeding back toward the system they'd arrived from.

Cheering broke out, with the CIC crew turning and congratulating each other, probably in spite of themselves. They quickly checked themselves, especially when they noticed Thatcher's stern gaze.

"This isn't over yet," he said. "What's the status of our third target, Ops?"

"She's streaming fuel and debris, but still appears operational. The other four ships are giving chase, with the one we struck limping behind."

Thatcher nodded.

"Shall I bring us about, Captain?" Sullivan asked, eagerness infusing his voice. He twisted in his seat to look at Thatcher.

"Negative. Set a new course for the jump gate into Nemorous."

"We're…running, sir? Deeper into the region?"

"We're following orders," Thatcher said, eyes locked onto his Nav officer's. "And we're not asking any questions."

Crestfallen, Sullivan turned back to his station. "Aye, sir."

Heading into the next system represented a risk, given there could be more enemy ships lying in wait there, maybe even the Xanthic. But Thatcher considered the risk small. These pirates were banding together in a way that was unprecedented for the Dawn Cluster—which meant they would proceed with some caution, knowing they had only Reardon Interstellar to back them up in the event of a backlash. If indeed Reardon was behind all this.

Either way, Thatcher considered the risk of entering Nemorous a tiny one. The pirates wouldn't split their forces. They would fight all together, or flee together. And if the Xanthic were still here, they would have already revealed themselves.

Right now, Thatcher's dirty trick had pissed off the pirates enough to chase him with abandon. They knew they still had the numerical superiority, and now that he'd expended his ploy with the missiles, he had no chance of defeating all five of their warships at once.

But I won't have to, will I?

Having accelerated constantly across half the system, the *Jersey* had an enormous head start on the pirate vessels, and now they were each maxing out their engines in their fervor to catch up with him. Thatcher had made a careful study of Vaughn's engagement with them, and he'd seen what a motley assortment of mismatched warships and converted freight haulers they were piloting. Typical for pirates, but it meant that each of their ship's acceleration profiles was different. As such, they were currently stringing themselves across the Gyve System in a ragged line, with the most powerful engine at the front, and the wounded ship in the rear, with several thousand kilometers between each ship already. And those gaps were expanding.

"Lower shields," Thatcher said as they neared the jump gate. "Nav, I suggest you triple-check your course calculations. We're sailing straight through the gate and we're not stopping."

"Aye, sir," Sullivan said, his tone gloomy.

"Ops, can you get a read on the gate at this distance while we're moving? I want to make it look like we're in such a panic that we didn't take the time to ping it."

"I've already run diagnostics, sir. The gate's fully functional." It was to Guerrero's credit that she didn't question or hesitate in executing her captain's orders. He knew it wasn't advised to transition through a jump gate at their current velocity, but battles involved risks, and he couldn't afford to appear at all relaxed to the pirates. If he did, they might sniff out what was coming and regroup.

"Candle?" Thatcher said, not bothering to spell out what he wanted. The man should know.

And he did. "Inertial compensators passed their checks, sir."

"Very good."

"Jumping now," Guerrero said, and a moment later the *Jersey* lurched forward, though it wasn't quite as noticeable as it usually was. The compensators worked together with their already considerable speed to make their ride just a little smoother.

"Nav, I want you to take us out of the jump zone once we enter Nemorous, and then bring us about. XO, keep shields down unless I say otherwise, and stand by to use our primary to hose down the shields of the first ship to come through. I also want a Hellborn loaded in the tube."

Both officers bent to their stations, and by the time the *New Jersey* emerged into the Nemorous System, they both were ready to execute. Thatcher allowed himself a satisfied nod as his ship slowed at a rate that would keep him within firing range of the entire jump zone.

A regular jump zone like this one spanned a thousand square kilometers, and regional jump zones were even bigger. Where in the zone you ended up after using the corresponding jump gate was essentially random, but the chances of one ship jumping on top of another were vanishingly small, and the jump gate's computer did what it could to cut down on those odds even more.

Though large, jump zones were still manageable enough that it was possible to keep the entire area under a waiting ship's guns. Which was exactly what Thatcher would do now.

"Sullivan, prepare a course that can be adapted depending on where the first ship appears—one that takes us past it at fifty percent engine power, the moment it shows up."

"Aye, sir."

The fastest pirate ship was one of the converted freighters, and it wasn't likely to have missiles—just some automated railgun turrets welded onto her hull. By moving perpendicular to those turrets, thereby increasing the *Jersey*'s transverse velocity relative to them, it would make their ship harder to hit. There was a good chance the cruiser would neutralize the pirate ship while remaining unscathed.

And indeed, when the converted freighter appeared, that was exactly what happened. It wasn't necessary to launch the Hellborn loaded in the *New Jersey*'s tube—instead, the starboard-side gunners pelted the freighter with their beams until it burst apart under the energy being dumped into it.

So it went for each subsequent pirate ship that entered the system. Their surprise was evident in their slow reaction time, and the *New Jersey* made short work of them, using only two missiles in the process, and relying on her primary and secondary lasers as well as her own railgun turrets to do the rest.

When the fifth ship went down—the one they'd already wounded with missiles, which exploded before it could fire a single shot—a stunned silence settled over the CIC. Had any light armored cruiser ever managed to dispatch seven foes in a single engagement? Thatcher had never heard of it happening.

News of the tactics he'd used would no doubt spread across the Cluster, no matter how he tried to keep a lid on them, and captains would begin to prepare against them. He doubted that could be helped.

No matter. I'll come up with new ones.

"Take us back to Gyve, Nav," he said. "Let's rendezvous with our eWar ship and then start toward Oasis to report our success."

As his officer carried out his orders, Thatcher scrutinized his own holoscreen, where there was still no sign of the Xanthic.

Where did you go?

Part of him felt relieved the massive vessel hadn't been with the pirates, this time. Another, slightly less sane part, felt disappointed.

CHAPTER TWELVE

Aboard the *New Jersey*
Omnist System, Tempore Region
Earth Year 2290

THE HATCH BUZZED, AND THATCHER THUMBED OPEN THE LOCK. Ensign Jimmy Devine stepped into the office to stand at rigid attention.

"At ease," Thatcher said.

Devine's left leg parted from his right as he folded his hands behind his back.

"Have a seat, Devine."

The young engineer did so, and Thatcher toyed with the idea of offering him a drink from the scotch Captain Vaughn had kept in the bottom drawer of his desk. He instantly scrapped the idea, since it ran counter to his recent restriction on fraternization as well as his intention of making this vessel a dry one.

"How is the crew reacting to our recent engagement?" Thatcher asked.

His informant shifted in his chair, as he always did before giving his captain news that was bad, or at best mixed. "You can tell they have a great deal of admiration for what you did, sir. I'm not sure anyone's wrapped their head around it yet, exactly. All the same, they sure are stingy with their praise. They don't like to see their prize money going to charity for at least the next month, and I take it their old captain would have stopped to salvage those wrecks, rather than leaving them for another Frontier vessel to come out and pick over."

Or for other pirates, if they come across the wrecks first. The *Jersey* was nearly halfway through her first month of donating any prize money she accrued. They'd left the Gyve System over a week ago, and would soon enter Dupliss. Barring any delays, they'd reach Oasis in a matter of days.

What Devine was telling him lined up with his own observations, along with the way most crewmembers clammed up when he tried to engage them in dialog. It was much the same with his department heads. They did as he asked, and he could tell they were pleased with the *Jersey*'s incredible performance. But there was no color to anything they said. No attempt to build the rapport necessary between a CIC crew, if they were to run a truly exceptional warship.

We can't rely on novel tactics in every single engagement. At some point, it's going to come down to the hearts and minds of the crew. If they haven't embraced their duty by then, we'll all perish.

Until now, Frontier had relied on being the biggest dog in the neighborhood. Thatcher didn't think that would continue to fly. Not with pirates presenting an increasingly united front, and even joining up with the Xanthic, the aliens' mysterious absence from the recent battle aside.

"How are you, Devine? Are you settling in well?"

The engineer nodded. "Yes, but—almost too well. I don't like pretending to agree with the others when they complain about you, sir. It grates on me."

"I'm afraid you'll have to continue, for the time being."

Devine had become an even better interface for the *Jersey*'s crew than the Command Master Chief, who often withheld the crew's true feelings from Thatcher, likely with good intentions. But with Devine regularly getting called to the captain's office, apparently to be reprimanded, it made him the perfect audience for all the crew's grievances. Which the ensign then relayed directly to his captain.

"Do you find there to be much of a contrast between serving in the Fleet and serving on the *Jersey*?"

"Oh, yes, sir. There are corners cut aboard the *Jersey* that would never fly on a Fleet ship. But things have gotten better since we first arrived. You really are changing things, if you don't mind my saying, sir."

Thatcher nodded. *Changing them for the better...for now. But I still don't know the extent of what this crew is capable of. Good or bad.*

The com lying on his desktop buzzed, and he snatched it up, with less self-control than he would have liked. As they drew closer to the wormhole that lay at the Dawn Cluster's center, connecting the Cluster to Earth Local Space, he was growing desperate to hear news from humanity's home planet. Had the Xanthic been scoured from the planet? Were the lunar colonies still secure?

Was Lin safe?

"Thatcher," he said into the microphone after lifting the device to his ear.

"Captain," Lucy Guerrero said, sounding thoroughly shaken.

"Yes? What is it?"

"It...the wormhole, sir."

"The wormhole? What about it?"

"We just received word...a passing mining vessel, sir... and..." Guerrero cleared her throat. "The wormhole to Earth has collapsed."

CHAPTER THIRTEEN

Aboard the *New Jersey*
Freedom System, Dupliss Region
Earth Year 2290

BEFORE JUMPING INTO THE FREEDOM SYSTEM, THATCHER HAD
called his first watch on duty three hours early, so that he would
have his best officers in the CIC as the *New Jersey* approached
Planet Oasis.

He didn't do that lightly. His crew was only large enough for
two twelve-hour watches, a reality enforced by the limited
number of bunks in the berthing compartment. As it was, every
enlisted member of the crew was forced to hot rack with another
crewmember, going to sleep in the same bunk just as the other
was getting up.

The cruiser had been designed that way to make room for
more weapon modules, but it made for long watches and spotty
sleep.

The wormhole's collapse wasn't the only news the mining
vessel had carried: shortly after word of the catastrophe spread
throughout the Cluster, Reardon Interstellar had shut down the

Freedom System and declared that all Frontier vessels were barred from the Dupliss Region, due to evidence that Frontier Security had been conspiring with pirates to enslave the people of Oasis.

"Ridiculous," Billy Candle had said when Thatcher had rooted him from his cabin to discuss the news. "They're moving against us based on an accusation that's true about *them*, not us. Those bastards."

"Language," Thatcher had said. He felt just as angry as Candle did, though he was surprised at the forcefulness of his XO's response. *Maybe he does take some pride in serving on a Frontier ship after all.*

Ever since he'd heard about the wormhole, Thatcher could barely concentrate. He wanted nothing more than to make way for the Sunrise System at full speed, and once there to reassemble the wormhole with his bare hands if he needed to.

I have to remain sensible. The UNC would get the wormhole back open. In the meantime, he needed to focus on the mission Admiral Faulkner had given him: stabilize the Dawn Cluster. It was still humanity's best hope for defeating the Xanthic.

Provided we'll ever see Earth again. Oh, God. I'm sixty thousand light years away from her... He shook his head to clear away those thoughts. *If I keep thinking like that, I'll go insane.*

They will *reopen the wormhole. They have to.*

"A battle group of Reardon ships is moving out from Oasis to meet us, sir," Guerrero said, her hands shaking as they moved across her console. "Ten strong." The lieutenant was usually somewhat jumpy, but ever since hearing that Reardon had virtually taken Oasis Colony hostage, she'd been a mess. She had a husband and two young children living on the planet.

At least you're on the same side of the galaxy as your family. But Thatcher knew that wasn't fair. Guerrero was hurting just as much as he was.

"Maintain course," Thatcher said. "Do what you can to establish contact with Veronica Rose, Ops."

"Aye, sir. The Reardon battle group is forming up around the nearest Helio base."

"Send them a transmission to the effect that we mean them no harm." Not that they could do much harm, even if they wanted to, with ten state-of-the-art warships arrayed against them and more scattered throughout the system.

Helio bases formed the backbone of industry throughout the Dawn Cluster. There, a captain could avail of any number of services, usually including dry dock repair, refitting, inter- and intra-corporate communications, and the purchase of anything from upgraded weapons to starship insurance.

Each base boasted multiple batteries of automated turrets. Six Helio bases surrounded Oasis, all in geostationary orbit. Controlling all six offered a strong defensive position—a position which, it seemed, Reardon Interstellar had secured for itself.

"Nav, calculate a deceleration profile that puts us just inside the range necessary for real-time communication. Coordinate with Ops to do so, if needed. Send your course to the *Squall*, and have them do the same."

"Aye, sir."

Once the *Jersey* came to a halt, it didn't take long for the largest Reardon battleship—a destroyer named the *Eagle*—to hail them. Thatcher told Guerrero to accept the call.

A wiry man appeared in the main holographic tank at the CIC's fore. This would be Ramon Pegg, CEO of Reardon Interstellar and captain of the company's flagship, the *Eagle*.

The holotank would render someone in 3D, so long as they were surrounded by the proper sensors—otherwise the entire thing would turn opaque, its front surface acting as a 2D screen. Either way, the person's image was blown up large, to give everyone in the CIC a clear view.

Pegg did have the right sensors. The holotank showed every

detail of his appearance in high resolution. His bald head, gleaming under the halogens. His bushy eyebrows. And his worm-like lips.

"Commander Thatcher, I presume?" Pegg's nonchalant tone seemed in contradiction with the way his thin shoulders bunched.

"Indeed. And you are Ramon Pegg, I take it." He wasn't sure whether Reardon used ranks, so he didn't attempt to use one. He saw no epaulet on Pegg's shoulders, or any other indication of rank.

"Your presence here is in violation of space safeguarded by the Oasis Protectorate," Pegg said. "I must strongly request that you leave at once."

"Frontier Security is a vital member of the Oasis Protectorate, Mr. Pegg. As such, this being a Frontier vessel, we have every right to be here."

"Your *company*, Commander, has been found guilty of conspiracy with pirates, with the aim of enslaving the good people of Oasis."

Thatcher cleared his throat loudly. "I hope you'll excuse me if I call what you're saying preposterous. We are Americans, largely, and so are the people living on Oasis. Americans do not enslave other Americans, as a rule."

"There is evidence."

"May I see it?"

Pegg's lips firmed, whitening with the pressure. "We are not the police, Commander. We are not a judge, or a jury. The civilian government on Oasis hired us to do a job, and that job is to protect them from threats such as yourself. We will not endanger them by pretending it would be meaningful to hold a trial here in space, so close to the planet. If you will not leave, then the threat you represent will be removed by force. We will destroy you, Commander."

"I think I see what you're getting at," Thatcher said. Clearly, Pegg was content to use the flimsiest pretext to oust Frontier from the Dupliss Region—territory his company had now effectively conquered.

In the meantime, Lucy Guerrero was gesturing at him, and he turned toward her, eyebrows raised. "Yes, Lieutenant?"

Instead of answering verbally, she sent a text message to his eyepiece. "Veronica Rose is trying to contact us," it read.

Nodding, he returned his gaze to Pegg. "Mr. Pegg, if you'll excuse me for a moment—"

Pegg reddened. "Commander Thatcher, if you do not take my words seriously, I will be—"

He cut the man off, ending their conversation with a tap on his console. "Put her through, Guerrero."

A second later, a 3D visual of Veronica Rose's head and shoulders appeared in the tank, her beauty a stark contrast to Pegg. "Commander," she said, sounding a little breathless. "Thank God you've returned. If we're to take any action against Reardon at all, we first need to evacuate Frontier's personnel from the planet, along with as many assets as we can. Until we do that, the entire company is effectively held hostage. I know there's nothing you can do with just the *Jersey*, but if you can return to the north and find other Frontier ships, then return here with them in good time, perhaps that will at least be enough firepower to force Reardon to the bargaining table. I can give you our ship's probable locations, and you—"

"I don't think that's necessary, Ms. Rose."

She narrowed her eyes, and the makings of a scowl began to take shape on her face. "What? Why not?"

"I believe we can evacuate all of Frontier's assets today."

"Explain."

"Pegg knows he's treading on very uncertain ground. The wormhole collapsed mere days ago, and for all he knows the UNC could get it reopened this evening. Then there are whatever UNC super-ships that were already in the Dawn Cluster. If word gets out that Reardon is openly attacking Frontier ships—which it will, if they do it in plain sight of Oasis—there's a good chance this system will be full of UNC warships within the week. Pegg's already playing with fire by ousting us from the Protectorate without producing any evidence. He won't take on any more risk before he gains a better understanding of the situation throughout the Cluster. So the time to evacuate is now, before Reardon figures out its footing."

Rose's shoulders rose and fell. "That seems to make sense. But you also may have misjudged Pegg. You realize, if we attempt this, it's the *New Jersey* and her crew that will bear the risk?"

"I do. But that's what warships are for." He noticed a couple of his CIC crew shifting uncomfortably in their seats at that. Candle, for his part, sat perfectly motionless.

"I'd better get back on the line with Pegg," he said. "I expect to see you soon, Ms. Rose."

"Good luck, Commander."

"Thank you." He ended the transmission and ordered Guerrero to reestablish contact with the destroyer.

"How *dare* you keep me waiting at such a sensitive time, Commander? Do you care so little for the lives of Oasis' population?"

"I care deeply for them," Thatcher said. "Which is why I intend to comply fully with your requirement."

In a heartbeat, Pegg's look of anger converted to one of confusion. "Oh? Well, good."

"Indeed. To do so, however, we will of course need time to evacuate our personnel and assets from the planet's surface."

Pegg's hand rose into the display, and he made a cutting gesture with it. "Out of the question."

"Then the *New Jersey* will not be leaving, and neither will the *Squall*, or the Frontier ships that will no doubt accumulate in this system as they report back."

His words earned him a glare of pure hatred. Clearly, Pegg

was not used to this level of pushback from anyone. "I will get back to you in a moment," he said, disappearing from the holotank.

He returned in less than a minute later. "You will be given no more than one Earth day to leave this system with everything you can transport," he said. "After that, if you are not gone, we will be forced to open fire on your vessels."

Thatcher doubted that was anything more than an empty threat, but it did surprise him a little that he made it. "I understand, Mr. Pegg. We will leave within twenty-four hours."

"Then I suggest you make haste, Commander. The clock is ticking."

CHAPTER FOURTEEN

Aboard the _New Jersey_
Freedom System, Dupliss Region
Earth Year 2290

"Well, Commander," Veronica Rose said as they stood a few meters from the workstation she'd set up amidst the _New Jersey_'s limited cargo space. "It seems O'Malley did well to recruit you. Doing so might prove to be the peak of his career."

"O'Malley," Thatcher repeated, his eyes wandering to the blocky desk taking up space in the corner of his already-cramped cargo bay. The _Jersey_'s load master was not likely to celebrate the CEO setting up an office here. "How is Mr. O'Malley?"

"I'm not sure. As far as I know, he's trapped on the other side of the wormhole for the time being, in Earth Local Space. I haven't spoken with him in months."

"Pity," he said, returning his gaze to Rose's porcelain face. Then his eyes wandered back to the desk as he fought a frown that was tugging at the corners of his mouth.

"Securing our exit from Freedom System, singlehandedly

SCOTT BARTLETT

defeating seven pirate ships…” Rose shook her head. “It seems you *are* a miracle worker.”

He chuckled at that, a little sardonically, and forgot the desk for a moment. “A great writer once said that any sufficiently advanced technology is indistinguishable from magic. I would say the same for tactics. Given the current state of space warfare, it isn’t difficult to be advanced.”

Rose smiled broadly, clearly impressed and maybe a little amused at Thatcher’s sweeping statement. “I can tell that having me aboard perturbs you, Commander.”

“Hmm?” he said, jerking his gaze from the desk once more and back to her emerald eyes. “Oh. Not at all, Ms. Rose, I assure you.”

“Then maybe it’s the idea of my holding court inside your cargo bay. Don’t worry, I won’t monopolize the space. And unless I’m holding a sensitive meeting, I won’t bar your crew from it.”

Unless you’re holding a sensitive meeting, Thatcher thought, the words echoing in his mind. He cleared his throat. “I’m sure the arrangement will be very workable. Very workable. You and Lieutenant Nacar will get along well.” Nacar was the *New Jersey*’s load master, and the fact Rose was his boss was the only reason he’d tolerate this situation.

Thatcher brushed an imaginary piece of lint from his service uniform’s sleeve and forced himself to take a deep breath. *Veronica Rose is your boss, and you need to be accommodating,* he told himself. *You can’t treat this as an enemy boarding action.* However much it felt like one.

At least the *Jersey* wouldn’t be giving up any of her weaponry, as the *Squall* was. They’d managed to talk Reardon into letting them use one of the Helio bases surrounding Oasis to modify the eWar ship. Currently, the *Squall* had so many weapons pointed at her that Thatcher would be very jumpy, were

90

he one of her crew. He doubted the modifications would take less than twenty-four hours, but he also doubted Reardon would actually enforce their deadline by firing on the eWar ship once their time ran up. *Hopefully not....*

They were taking advantage of the Gladius combat system's modular nature to quickly remove a capacitor section, the small arms locker, and an ammo storage module, all of which would be replaced by cargo bays. That would be where most of Frontier's evacuated personnel would be housed, along with as much company equipment as would fit. Both the *Squall*'s single shuttle and the *Jersey*'s pair of attack shuttles were busily ferrying people and gear out of Oasis' gravity well as quickly as they could manage.

Thatcher hated to relinquish firepower in the form of laser charge and ammo, but he knew it wouldn't limit his options in combat too badly. EWar ships didn't normally engage enemies directly anyway.

Rose walked to her desk, then turned to lean back against it. She wore a form-fitting blazer over a white collared shirt, and Thatcher wanted to frown again at how attractive she looked, even in formal attire. *I hope the crew doesn't get distracted by having such a good-looking woman on board.* Every branch of the U.S. military had been mixed-gender for centuries, but Rose's wintry beauty was something different—like she'd stepped directly off a fashion show runway and onto a warship.

"At times like this, I wish I could ask my father's advice," she said, staring across the cargo bay, her eyes wandering over stacked crates of ordnance, batteries, repair drone parts, and countless other necessities. "I used to accuse him of grooming me to take over Frontier since the day I said my first word, and I don't think that was far from the truth. But I'm not sure anything could have prepared me for this."

Thatcher stood there, his arms hanging uselessly at his sides.

He felt a need to reassure her—to suggest that the UNC would reopen the wormhole soon. But that would feel like a lie, since he had no idea what was going on with the wormhole. A large part of him stridently insisted—had been insisting ever since he'd heard the news—that opening or closing or doing *anything* with a wormhole was well beyond human technology. They'd found it open, and they'd used it for over a century, and now it was closed. Neither state was likely to change from human action.

But he pushed that voice to the back of his mind, where it needed to stay if he was to keep his sanity. If the wormhole didn't reopen, then he would remain a galaxy away from his wife. That wasn't an outcome he was willing to entertain.

"Even if they reopen the wormhole," Rose said, as though she'd been following the train of Thatcher's thought, "there's still the Xanthic. We'll all have to confront them sooner or later, I think. In the meantime, if the pirates really are forming their own corps, maybe even their own alliances…." She shook her head. "Trouble is only starting in the Dawn Cluster. There are plenty of other Reardons here, too. Corps that will keep pushing the boundaries of what they can get away, all the way to making open war on law-abiding corps, if the UNC lets them."

"They won't."

"How can you know that? If the wormhole stays closed, the entire game changes, Commander. The UNC won't be able to call for reinforcements, meaning the super-ships they have here are what they have, and that's it. They won't be able to maintain order if corps all across the Cluster start misbehaving as Reardon has. And they will. Mark my words. Having the exclusive right to mine and develop a system is too tempting a boon to any corporation's bottom line. It's well worth it to win that right by force, if they can."

Thatcher nodded slowly. He couldn't find any fault with

what Rose was saying. *Things are about to get very interesting, aren't they?* "What do you want to do, then?"

She shrugged. "What else is there? We have to go to Clime. To free Oasis Colony from Reardon's grip, we need the UNC's help."

CHAPTER FIFTEEN

Aboard the *New Jersey*
Sunrise System, Clime Region
Earth Year 2290

"Good Lord," Thatcher muttered as the entire CIC stared at the holotank, which was swimming with thousands of scale-model ships scattered across the size-adjusted representation of the Sunrise System.

"It looks like we have something of a wait ahead of us," Veronica Rose said from over his right shoulder.

He glanced back at her, trying not to appear annoyed. *Does she intend to stay there during engagements, too? I don't need her questioning my tactics, no matter how much she thinks she knows about military affairs.* Rose was buckled into one of the CIC's observations seats, which lacked armrests, and so she often gripped the straps running down her front. She was doing so now, and her posture put Thatcher in mind of an overly enthusiastic schoolgirl.

As for the sheer number of ships here, he'd expected something like it, if not quite this quantity. After the *Jersey* had passed from the Dupliss Region into Unity, they began to encounter increasing numbers of starships the closer they drew to Clime, all headed to the UNC's Dawn Cluster headquarters in Sunrise. Without exception, every ship they met bore some sort of grievance against a rival corporation, and they all wanted the UNC to intervene.

"Nothing we've heard so far comes close to our dilemma," Rose had said from her observation seat as the *Jersey* prepared to jump to the fourth Unity system along her journey. "Civilian lives hang in the balance, back on Oasis. The UNC *has* to do something."

Thatcher hoped she was right, in part because his crew's morale had sunk low. Some of them had family on Oasis, like Guerrero, but more of them had their homes in Earth Local Space, and talk of whether they'd ever see their loved ones again had largely replaced the complaints about prize money. *One small blessing, I guess.*

At Rose's suggestion, he'd held an ice cream social on the mess decks as they neared Clime Region. Initially he'd been resistant to the idea, but the crew *had* done well in the recent engagement, in spite of themselves. He'd also spotted an opportunity, and had embraced the event whole-heartedly, which he turned into a cocktail party two hours in.

Two mess specialists wheeled in carts laden with booze, and everyone happily went to work on them—the *Jersey*'s crew and officers, along with officers from the *Squall* as well as Frontier executives, who'd been shuttled over from the accompanying eWar ship. It made for plenty of dragging feet the next day, but little was likely to happen in the cold regions anyway, and Thatcher saw the massive consumption as a great victory in his war to turn the *New Jersey* into a dry vessel. First the booze had to be disposed of, after all, and if it spiked crew morale in the short-term, all the better.

"Sullivan, set a course for the nearest UNC Helio base,"

Thatcher ordered. "Tell the *Squall* to wait for us here, just outside the jump zone." He eyed the holotank with unease, his focus resting on the empty space on Sunrise's distant outskirts, where the wormhole had been. The UNC had apparently dragged one of its Helio bases out there, no doubt to act as a staging area for its efforts to reopen the gateway between the Cluster and Earth Local Space. But there was no trace of the wormhole that the *Jersey*'s sensors could detect.

Thatcher's stomach sank toward his feet. *If we could reopen that wormhole, then we probably wouldn't be far from opening wormholes wherever we want, to wherever we want. But we're nowhere near reopening it, are we?*

The UNC knew that, he felt sure. They had to try, of course —if only to maintain the appearance of order for as long as possible. But they were going to fail, and soon everyone would learn of that failure. The Dawn Cluster stood on its own, perhaps forever. The humans here might as well belong to a separate species. And the people back home...prey for the Xanthic.

Lin. No. I will return to you. I'll find a way. He couldn't see how he would succeed where the UNC's best scientists would surely fall short. But he also didn't care. *I will find a way.*

They fell in with the dozens of ships surrounding one of the Helio bases orbiting Sunrise's third planet, a cloud-covered rock that reminded him of Venus. The UNC maintained hundreds of Helio bases throughout the system, and they were all surrounded by corp ships waiting to have their grievances heard. All the while, massive UNC super-ships prowled—hulking fighter drone carriers and dreadnoughts that ran for kilometers from stem to stern, both which dwarfed the waiting starships.

The *New Jersey* was given a number when she arrived, forty-seven, and then told not to contact the base until they were contacted first, barring an emergency. Thatcher didn't dare leave the CIC, for fear that the UNC would skip right over them in the absence of the *Jersey*'s CO, forcing them to wait until after the ships with higher numbers had been dealt with. That could take forever.

Veronica Rose remained as well—it was arguably more important that she be here, after all.

"Sir, I don't see any shuttles moving to and from the Helio base," Guerrero remarked after a half hour had passed.

Thatcher nodded. "They must not be holding physical meetings. That's good for us, I suppose, since waiting for people to come and go from the base would take even longer."

"Nevertheless," Rose put in from behind him. "We'll request an in-person meeting."

"Hmm," Thatcher said, then fell silent, stifling a yawn.

His fatigue tugged at his eyelids and muddled his thoughts. Even though the journey from Oasis had been fairly uneventful, there'd been no shortage of stress and worry to go with the usual demands of being captain. Even during the most uneventful of times, his com could be counted on to disrupt his sleep at least a few times with its aggravating buzz. Course changes, strange behavior from other vessels, inconsistent jump gate readings— the interruptions were always legitimate issues that required the captain's attention. But they eroded his rest like the tide erodes the shore.

His grandfather had warned him about those sleep-shattering calls, and told him they posed the greatest threat to his enthusiasm for being captain. "It doesn't matter," he'd told his grandfather, just as idealistic youths always did. "It will be worth it." And it was worth it. But he felt very tired, all the same.

Their turn arrived at last, and when Guerrero put the transmission through, a man appeared inside the holotank wearing the midnight service dress uniform of the United Nations and Colonies. "Greetings, Captain…." The UNC officer looked down at something, probably a holoscreen. "Um, Vaughn. Of the Frontier Security ship the *New Jersey*. Is that correct?"

"You need to update your records," Veronica Rose said,

before Thatcher could speak. "Commander Tad Thatcher is now the CO of this unit."

Knowing she couldn't see him, Thatcher didn't bother to keep his lips from pressing together in a thin line. *I need to find a way to 'politely' exile her from my CIC.* Being superseded as the first to speak to an outside party aboard his own ship wasn't sitting well with him at all.

"Apologies, madam." The UNC officer blinked in confusion. He wouldn't be able to see Rose, after all—for the purposes of communication, the CIC's sensors all pointed to the captain's chair. "I am Lieutenant Laurence Klein, with the UNC. What brings—"

"We're here to make a report about a troubling situation taking shape in the Dupliss Region," Thatcher said, cutting Klein off to ensure that he spoke next. "Reardon Interstellar has barred Frontier Security from the region, based on the evidence-free claim that our company has been working with pirates to somehow harm or enslave the population of Oasis Colony, which we were hired to protect. The main irony is that we have good reason to believe Reardon, in fact, has been consorting with pirates. Either way, until challenged, they have effectively conquered the Dupliss Region for their own exploitation. We're here to request the UNC's aid in liberating the people of Oasis as well as the other American colonies throughout Dupliss."

"I see. Well, Commander, it is regrettable for me to inform you that until the wormhole is reopened, the UNC can offer no aid beyond Clime, Unity, Basin, Sunlit Mesa, and Steppe Mortalis—those regions commonly known as 'cold' regions. Anyone, whether corporate employee or civilian, is welcome to shelter inside one of the systems that comprise those regions. But at present, the only way we can guarantee the cold regions' security is to keep all of our vessels within them. I hope you understand."

"I don't understand," Rose cut in, and this time Thatcher

didn't begrudge her the interruption. "I can't see how you can leave millions of civilian lives hanging in the balance so casually. Those people have been effectively stripped of their freedoms, and until Reardon's grip on Dupliss is broken, they're living in what amounts to a corporate dictatorship!"

Klein shifted uncomfortably. "It is regrettable, madam. But I can only follow orders. There is nothing to be done, at present."

"Can we have an in-person meeting?"

"I am afraid that won't be possible, given the volume of ships waiting to—"

"The UNC was given the power it has in order to safeguard all of humanity." Rose's voice was like cold steel. "*All* of it. I hope you know that you're failing in that duty."

"I do not know what to say," Klein said.

"To hell with you. Cut off the transmission, Commander."

CHAPTER SIXTEEN

Aboard the *New Jersey*
Sunrise System, Clime Region
Earth Year 2290

THATCHER NODDED TO GUERRERO, CONFIRMING ROSE'S ORDER to terminate the transmission. He was certain it wasn't a good idea to mouth off to the UNC, but then, he felt just as upset as Rose.

"Commander," the CEO said with barely restrained emotion. "Can I speak with you for a minute?"

He nodded. "Candle, you have the conn. Take us away from the Helio base—climb to a higher orbit."

"Aye, sir."

Rose followed him into the conference room, just off the CIC. He held the hatch open for her and closed it again once she was seated. Then he made his way around the table and sat opposite her, folding his hands on the tabletop. "Yes, Ms. Rose?"

"Do I need to remind you who is CEO of this corp, Commander?"

Other than a slight narrowing of his eyes, he didn't answer.

"What was the meaning of you taking the lead in the discussion with Klein?"

"I believe you took the lead," he said, regarding her levelly. "You were the first to speak."

"Then *you* jumped in and gave him a stripped-down version of events. You should know that my father had me trained in *everything* needed to run a private military, from ops to logistics to effective messaging. Rhetoric, Commander. The art of using language to elicit emotion."

"I see." Thatcher wasn't sure where she was going with this.

She heaved a ragged sigh, pressing her face into an open palm. *This is the first time I've seen her lose her cool.*

When she lifted her head again to look at him, she appeared more composed. "You're a military man, Commander. A ship's captain now, and a damned good one. Quite possibly the best natural captain I've seen—judging from your single engagement, anyway. But there are certain things you know nothing about. Things I was trained extensively in. Those things, you must leave to me."

A silence stretched between them, and eventually Rose's eyebrows jerked up. She obviously expected a response, but he wanted to carefully consider his words.

"I can agree there are matters that should be left to you," he said at last. "Many things, most likely. And in this instance, I think we should have worked out a plan in advance—who would say what, and when. But one thing I *cannot* have is my authority being undermined inside my own CIC, in front of my officers. A captain should be the first to speak when hailed by an outside party, for example—not someone who isn't even in the *New Jersey*'s chain of command. You're my boss, and I must do as you direct. But at the micro-level, the day-to-day operations of my ship...that must be left to me."

Incredibly, Rose nodded. "Maybe it's best for me to keep away from the CIC, to avoid the temptation to micromanage you and your crew. You're right, Commander. This is your ship, and you must have full command of her. I'll give you direction, and then you will carry out my orders in the way you consider most effective. The exception being any time it would be advantageous for me to speak to an outside party, like today."

For a moment, he sat there, stunned. He hadn't expected such a reasonable reception for his concerns. "Thank you, Ms. Rose. This seems very fair."

She nodded curtly, and as she did his com buzzed.

He tapped the button to activate speaker mode, so that Rose could hear as well. "Thatcher."

"Sir," Guerrero said, "we're being hailed by a destroyer registered to Sunder Incorporated."

Thatcher exchanged glances with Rose. Here was exactly the scenario they'd just discussed. "We'll be right out."

They drew a few curious glances as they reentered the CIC together, but that was nothing new. Since becoming captain, he'd grown used to everyone's eyes following him everywhere.

"Go ahead, Ops," he said as he settled into the padded leather command seat. "Put them in the tank."

A man appeared in the holotank, his eyes finding Thatcher's right away and regarding him as though he were a piece of spoiled meat. His gaze instantly put Thatcher on edge. "Yes?" he said.

"Commander Thatcher, is it not?" The stranger's voice was deep, and sounded so arrogant that Thatcher wondered if it was an act. The man was perfectly bald, with a white mustache and facial hair that extended down to run along his jaw, though the chin itself was bare.

"It is," Thatcher said, and gestured toward Rose, who stood beside the captain's chair, hands at her sides. "This is Veronica Rose, CEO of Frontier Security."

"I'm aware. I am Simon Moll, captain of the *Victorious* and CEO of Sunder Incorporated. I have a proposition for you, which

I would very much like to discuss in person. May I come aboard?"

Thatcher and Rose looked at each other. She gave a slight nod.

"You're welcome to dock a shuttle on our starboard side, Captain Moll," Thatcher said. "We'll receive you there."

Forty minutes later, Thatcher was back in the conference room, seated at the head of the table and watching Rose and Moll eye each other from opposite chairs. Even from a seated position, Moll seemed to tower. He was certainly much taller than Thatcher, who came a few inches shy of six foot.

"I've heard great things about your corporation, madame." Moll's was compliment diluted somewhat by his perpetual smirk. "Unlike most corps in the Cluster, you conduct yourself with some honor, or so I am told."

"Thank you," Rose said coolly, her eyes never leaving the other CEO's. "I've heard of your outfit as well."

The smirk broadened into a slight smile. "I doubt the reports you've heard about Sunder were quite as pristine. We have many enemies, and on occasion we've been forced to place expedience over honor."

Then you have no honor, Thatcher mused, but he kept the thought to himself.

"You must know we belong to the Oasis Protectorate," Rose said. "And that the only other private military company in the alliance is Reardon Interstellar."

"Yes," Moll said. "Their low opinion of us is mutual."

Something clicked in Thatcher's head, then. *The Sunder-Reardon Incident.* They'd taught it back in the academy, and he felt like kicking himself for not remembering sooner. It was the first intercorporate conflict to occur in the Dawn Cluster, and also the event that had caused the UNC to maintain such a large presence here—to police the Cluster and ensure corporations from every country could operate safely. *That was sixty years ago. Could Moll have been involved in that?* He racked his mind, but couldn't place the name in what he knew of the Incident. *He would have to be eighty at least, and he looks like a young sixty.* But it was possible. Cosmetic surgery and life extension tech worked greater wonders for some than it did for others.

"Did you know that Sunder tried for the same Oasis contract Reardon now holds?" Moll asked. "But your government wanted an American corp, of course, and it was easy to withhold the contract from us after Ramon Pegg began smearing our good name during the bidding process. In much the same way he's currently smearing yours."

Thatcher couldn't help himself. "What's your proposition?" Both CEOs looked at him, Rose's eyes widening meaningfully. But Thatcher just wanted Moll to get to the point. He couldn't tolerate his glib smugness for much longer.

Moll's eyes returned to Rose, and he gave a resonant chuckle. "Straight to business I see, Commander." His tone made it clear he was dismissing Thatcher out of hand. "Well, why not. Sunder has long had a contingency plan in place to prepare for a scenario in which the UNC no longer plays the role of 'Cluster police,' whether by choice or because they are unable. It seems that with the collapse of the wormhole, that contingency has arrived. Three other PMCs are party to the plan, one which Sunder shares an alliance with—the Daybreak Alliance—and two that belong to the Valkyrie Bloc. Efforts are already underway to bring those entire alliances fully on board."

Moll stopped talking, and this time he was clearly waiting to be asked. Stubbornly, Thatcher held his peace.

"What's the plan, then?" Rose said.

"I'll tell you. But first, I should warn you that our plan may not seem consistent with your principles—at least, not at first. With further consideration, though, I'm confident you'll see that Sunder Incorporated and its allies seek the exact same ends you do. Frontier wants stability in the Cluster, so that American colonists might prosper, and I happen to know that you were sent here by Rear Admiral Faulkner to achieve the exact same thing, Commander."

"How do you know that?" Moll's words felt like a bucket of ice water tossed in Thatcher's face.

The man's smirk briefly became a grin. "You'll find I know a great many unexpected things—and entering into a partnership with us will mean *you* know those things as well. But for now, the plan. Sunder and its partner corporations intend to secure the entire northwest of the Dawn Cluster as our power base. From there, we can work on stabilizing the rest of the Cluster. We can effectively control the northwest by locking down only four regions: Candor, Endysis, The Splay, and Dupliss. If you agree to help us execute our plan—entering into partnership with us, bearing the same risks and reaping the same benefits—then Sunder will gladly help you retake the Dupliss Region from Reardon. Under our plan, that region will be all yours, to harvest its fruits and to defend it, as it will be one of the four gateways into a northwest that will be controlled by our super-alliance."

Moll leaned back, then, apparently content to let that sink in. *He knows how to put on a show. I'll give him that.* The prospect the CEO-captain raised was intriguing, but Thatcher knew implementing this plan would not be a bloodless affair. Plenty of corporations occupying the space he proposed to take over wouldn't want to live under the rule of this new super-alliance.

"You mentioned knowing certain things," Rose said. " Thing others don't know. I'd like to hear an example, before I agree to anything. As a show of good faith."

Moll nodded without hesitation, and Thatcher got the sense he'd expected this. "Absolutely. How about this: the UNC recognizes that if the wormhole stays closed—which I think we all know it will—then improved communications will be vital, if there's to be any hope of peace. And so they're giving up one of the precious technologies they've kept from us for so long: instant comm units, one for every corporation. They're making them as tamper-proof as they can, to prevent corps from replicating them, but I can tell you my people will crack these things open sooner than later. So will others. Before too long, every ship in the Cluster will have instant communication, even across hundreds of light years."

"Why weren't we offered a unit when we spoke to the UNC?" Rose said, reproach creeping into her voice.

Perhaps because you told their representative to go to hell, Thatcher reflected.

Moll shrugged, his massive shoulders heaving. "For now, they're only giving them to corps who ask for them—corps in the know. They'll need to start mass-producing the units to meet demand, so this is how they're limiting numbers for the time being. If you ask for one, you'll get one."

Incredible. Instant comms would be another game-changer for space warfare. No one knew how the UNC had managed it, though the leading theory had something to do with entangled electrons. Verifying the theory had always been impossible, since the UNC cracked down on anyone who tried.

"I'm sure I don't need to tell you this alone will change everything," Moll said. "Soon, PR will be as vital as laser batteries for achieving a corp's ends—maybe *more* vital. Message your cause well, get the Cluster on your side, and doors will start opening. New allies, better intel. Weaponized scandals. The age of propaganda is about to begin."

Rose nodded, birthing a strange mix of emotion in Thatcher's gut. The Sunder CEO talked sense, Thatcher had to admit, however grudgingly. Moll's plan could lead to stability throughout the Cluster, and if Frontier refused his offer, they'd probably be resigning themselves to the sidelines of history.

Even so…anxiety tightened the base of his throat. It wasn't just the bloodshed the plan would entail. It was also that he hadn't trusted Moll since the moment the man appeared in his holotank.

"I'm ready to agree to your proposal," Rose said. "On one condition."

Simon Moll raised his eyebrows and waited.

"All throughout the space we help you conquer, civil liberties will be preserved, for all colonists. No more of the surveillance and censorship the UNC has visited on us for more than a century. Everyone living within our borders will be truly free."

Thatcher found himself nodding his approval. *So. She actually does care about American values.*

Moll appeared to give Rose's requirements due consideration, his fingers drumming on the conference table for several long seconds.

"Very well," he said. "We have a deal."

CHAPTER SEVENTEEN

Aboard the *New Jersey*
Sable System, Dupliss Region
Earth Year 2290

THE *NEW JERSEY* TOOK THE REGIONAL JUMP GATE INTO THE FIRST Dupliss system, her CIC crew on high alert.

"I have something, sir," Guerrero said a few minutes after they hit the jump zone.

Thatcher's hands tensed involuntarily, gripping his chair's armrests. "A Reardon ship?" He used his station's holoscreen to scan a scaled-down representation of the Sable System, searching for a hostile vessel. The influx of traffic toward Clime from the Cluster's periphery had slowed to a fraction of what it had been when they'd last flown through, but there were still a dozen ships in-system, approaching the regional jump gate from three different jump zones.

"Negative," Guerrero said. "I believe it's one of ours—the *Boxer*, a Frontier ship. A frigate. She appears damaged, traveling at a fraction of her normal cruising speed."

"Set a rendezvous course, Nav. Share it with the other three ships." In addition to the *Squall* and the *Victorious*, a Sunder logistics ship called the *Lightfoot* also accompanied them .

"Aye, sir."

Thatcher reached for the comm suspended in a holster down the side of his chair, withdrew his hand, then reached for it again. He thumbed the code for Veronica Rose and brought it to his ear.

"Veronica Rose."

"Ms. Rose. This is Thatcher."

"What can I do for you, Commander?"

"You may want to come up here. We've come across another Frontier vessel. She's badly damaged, from what we can tell at this distance."

"I'll be right up."

Soon, Rose was back in her observation seat, and Thatcher tried to ignore the sensation that her gaze was crawling across the back of his head, trying to penetrate his skull and study the brains underneath.

It took three hours to reach the frigate, even though both ships were headed straight for each other, each having noticed the other. The frigate's limping increased the transit time greatly.

If that ship had instant comms, there might be no need to rendezvous. Another testament to how the innovation would change things, once widespread. The *New Jersey*'s unit had yet to be fully integrated with the ship's systems, but once it was, Thatcher would be able to speak with reps from any Cluster corporation he wished, provided they also had a unit. Whether the new comm would enable communication with Earth had been the first thing Thatcher had asked the UNC officer who'd arranged for the comm's delivery to the *Jersey*, but apparently the thing lacked that kind of range. *They must not rely on entangled particles after all. Distance wouldn't matter, if they did.*

At least, he didn't think it would. Probably, he was kidding himself by thinking he had any real understanding of quantum physics.

Once they finally drew into real-time communication range with the frigate, a woman with a pleasant, youthful face appeared in the holotank, her blond hair drawn back tightly beneath her beige cap. "Hello, there," she said in a Southern drawl. "This is Commander Pat Frailey contacting you. Who do I have the pleasure of speaking with? I thought Captain Vaughn commanded the *Jersey*."

"Hello to you, Commander. I'm Commander Tad Thatcher. I'm afraid Captain Vaughn passed away from a heart attack during an engagement."

"Oh, no. Truly?" Tears sprang to Frailey's eyes, and she stared into space for a moment as she dabbed them with the tips of her fingers. "My gosh. I knew Vaughn for years. Everything's changing in the Cluster these days, ain't it? I'm sorry."

"No apology needed," Thatcher murmured, waiting for Frailey to compose herself.

"Commander Frailey, this is Veronica Rose. I'm aboard the *New Jersey* as well."

Frailey's mouth became an 'O,' her tears forgotten. "Ms. Rose? Heavens, what are you doing on there?"

"You're aware of Reardon Interstellar's recent behavior?"

"I know they wouldn't let me in the Freedom System at all. Called Frontier a bunch of pirates."

"Yes, well, Commander Thatcher here was kind enough to help me evacuate from Oasis Colony, along with all of our personnel that were in the system. He's also let me set up shop in his cargo bay."

"Well bless your heart, Commander."

"Was it a Reardon ship that fired on you, Pat?" Rose asked.

"No, ma'am. That was pirates, just one system back. Three of their scows were trying to take over Prosper Station, and we intervened. Didn't go so well for us." Frailey shook her head. "Dupliss is lousy with pirates right now, with Reardon keeping to the one system by all accounts, just letting the scumbags have their way with the people Reardon's meant to be protecting."

If Thatcher didn't have to twist around to meet Rose's gaze, he would have. By the sounds of things, the pirates were well on their way to cementing their own corporations and possibly even alliances, if they hadn't already. And Reardon was doing little to hide its association with those pirates, instead using them to occupy Dupliss.

It made sense, in a demented sort of way. With just the ships Reardon had, there would be no way for it to secure all of Dupliss against invaders coming from Unity, The Splay, Tempore, and Yu—the four regions from which Dupliss could be accessed. Indeed, if Frontier succeeded in taking back Dupliss with Sunder's help, then they too would need more ships to hold it.

But how would we get them? Thatcher could think of a number of ways, some more savory than others. Ideally, the UNC would give Frontier their nanofab tech, so the company could speed up its starship construction from years to months— weeks, in the case of smaller ships. Of course, first they'd need to waive their cap on how large corporate militaries were allowed to grow. But maybe the UNC could be convinced that favoring Frontier like that would help stabilize the Cluster.

Somehow, I think we have a long way to go before that happens.

Rose spoke up again. "Pat, have you encountered any…other warships in the area?"

Thatcher made sure to keep his expression neutral. He knew Rose was talking about the Xanthic, but the fact one of their ships had been encountered in the Cluster was still a secret. If that got out, the panic it caused could make a bad situation a lot worse.

"Other than Reardon's, and the pirates'? No, ma'am."

"How extensive is your damage, Commander?" Thatcher

said. "Is it anything a loan of our repair drones would help with?"

"I don't think so, but thanks all the same. They blew off half our stern, which took out one of our main thrusters. Nearly caused our reactor to go into meltdown—we managed to pull off an emergency restart with three ships blasting away at us, and they lost interest once we dragged ourselves far enough away."

The sound of Veronica Rose unstrapping herself from the observation seat reached Thatcher's ears, and next she was standing beside him, peering up into Frailey's enlarged face. "Commander, I want you to seek repairs at one of the Helio bases in this system. In the meantime, you're to watch out for any Frontier ships coming through. I suspect more will, as Reardon kicks them out of Freedom System. Reach out to them with my orders to stay put here in Sable, while seeing to any repairs they might need. I want my fleet fully operational, and stationed where I can reach them. Is that understood?"

"Yes, ma'am."

Rose turned to Thatcher. "Commander, please set a course for Epact System. Prosper Station is too important a trade hub to allow it to fall into pirate hands. Brief the *Squall*, *Victorious*, and *Lightfoot* on what's going on, and then meet me in the cargo bay. We have battle plans to discuss."

CHAPTER EIGHTEEN

Aboard the *New Jersey*
Epact System, Dupliss Region
Earth Year 2290

ENSIGN JIMMY DEVINE STRODE ACROSS ONE OF SEVERAL catwalks suspended over the *New Jersey*'s main engineering deck, bouncing a flow nozzle in the palm of his hand. One of the backup thruster's liquid hydrogen tanks wasn't feeding like it should, and he'd feel a lot better once it was back to normal. As long as the main thrusters were functioning, the issue wasn't likely to matter, but anything could happen in battle. If the larger thrusters went, then this little flow nozzle replacement could make the difference between victory and the entire crew perishing. *Probably won't, but it could.*

Devine was just glad the *Jersey* didn't have a fission reactor, like so many starships still did. Antimatter was about a bajillion times more stable, and while an engineer's job was still just as vital to the ship's success, he rested a little easier without hundreds of nuclei decaying somewhere near his head every second.

Of course, there was always the possibility of antimatter leaking out and coming into contact with regular matter *outside* of the propulsion system. If that happened, the annihilation would generate an explosion inside the ship, proportionate to the amount of escaped antimatter. That wouldn't be good. But the designers had installed plenty of failsafes to prevent it from happening, and engineers like Devine were here to make sure those failsafes stayed in good working order.

"...sure he thinks he's better than everyone," someone said from below, the snatch of dialog drifting up to reach Devine. "Maybe even Ms. Rose." He halted, realizing he was directly above Tony Jowers and Axel Navarro, two deck engineers. They didn't look up—his footsteps must have faded into the background hum of the engine room.

This was how he'd gathered everything he'd passed on to the captain. Not by eavesdropping, but from one-on-one conversations, with other crewmembers confiding their grievances in him when they thought no one else would hear. No one dared openly complain about Captain Thatcher. He had a growing number of fans among the crew, after all, and it only took one to report the complainer for sewing dissension. But his detractors seemed to be talking more often, with their complaints growing bolder.

To their eyes, Devine made a good confidant. They figured he had to hate the captain, given how much he was reprimanded by him. But he also sensed some hesitance on their part. Maybe because he was new, fresh from the Fleet. *I wonder what I'll hear now.* Jowers and Navarro were among Captain Thatcher's biggest detractors.

"What he did to the pirates was something else," Jowers was saying, in response to a remark from Navarro that Devine had missed. "But it isn't hard to tell he wants all the glory to himself. I don't believe for one second that keeping that battle plan from his officers was about OPSEC. It was about making sure they wouldn't get any of the credit. He acts all high and mighty, making out we're money-hungry, and donating our prize money to Oasis. But how's it any better to be obsessed with glory?"

Navarro spoke again, but he was doing a much better job than Jowers at keeping his voice down. Devine couldn't make out the words.

"Exactly," Jowers said. "That compromises our effectiveness just as much, and puts us all in danger. Just look at the situation we're in right now. Charging into another engagement with a bunch of pirates, while the other Frontier ships get to gather together and hang out in Sable. You think Captain Vaughn would have sailed into danger without waiting for the proper backup to show up? Not a chance. I tell ya, Axe, I'm asking Ms. Rose for a transfer off this ship the first chance I get. And if she won't get me it, I'll go work for someone else. Reardon, maybe. At least they have the sense to hunker down in one system and let others do the fighting for them."

"You idiots," Devine said, and he could hardly believe the words had left his mouth once he said them. He resisted the urge to clap a hand over his lips as Jowers and Navarro looked up to see him standing there, the flow nozzle replacement all but forgotten in his clenched fist. Their faces whitened.

"Devine?" Jowers said. "You—what'd you say?"

He knew he should try to walk his words back, but he couldn't force himself to do it. *I'm tired of playing the insubordinate ensign. Tired of pretending to agree as the others bash the captain.* "I said you're an idiot."

"Why?" Jowers said, his eyebrows bunched. "You heard what we said, I'm guessing. But Thatcher's been hardest on you out of anyone. You're not about to tell me you disagree."

"Yeah, I am, actually. You got a big problem, Jowers, and I'll tell you what it is. Your attitude's all twisted. This company's been spoiled with soft targets for way too long. Frontier's gotten by on superior weaponry, and better ships, so dealing with any pirates you stumbled on was like shooting fish in a barrel. But it ain't like that anymore. The wormhole's closed, and it might not ever open again. The UNC ain't gonna hold your hand no more. Pirates are forming their own corps, now, and PMCs have free reign to get violent if they want to. There's no one left to tuck you in and tell you everything's gonna be all right."

Jowers' face grew harder with every word, and Navarro's was completely blank. There was none of the jocularity they'd shown Devine since he'd joined the *Jersey*'s company. That stung, a little, but he was too riled up to stop now.

"From now on, anyone in the Cluster who doesn't run a tight ship is screwed. So are you, if you transfer to a corp that shrinks from a fight. You're lucky Thatcher took command of the *Jersey*. You won the lottery with him. You'll realize that soon enough— hopefully it won't be after you transfer to a ship where they run things sloppy, a ship doomed to get turned into space dust."

With that, Devine turned and marched the rest of the way across the catwalk, leaving Jowers and Navarro wearing expressions that mixed shock and anger. His stomach turned over as he entered the next compartment, and his head felt light.

I screwed up, didn't I? He'd just removed himself as a valuable source of intel for the captain. All because he couldn't keep his big mouth shut.

CHAPTER NINETEEN

Aboard the *New Jersey*
Epact System, Dupliss Region
Earth Year 2290

THATCHER CLOSELY MONITORED THE TACTICAL DISPLAY ON HIS holoscreen as the small formation of Frontier and Sunder ships drew closer to the rocky red planet whose moon Prosper Station orbited

"Adjust course two degrees to starboard, Nav," Thatcher said. "Ops, share the new heading with our accompanying vessels."

"Aye, sir."

It was the third course adjustment he'd made since entering Epact, all in response to maneuvers made by the three pirate scows surrounding the station. *'Scow' probably isn't the right word, here.* For pirate ships, these vessels were above average in size and firepower. Even though the Frontier and Sunder warships outnumbered them four-to-three, they could possibly put up a strong fight, especially considering the *Squall* and the *Lightfoot* didn't have much in the way of weaponry.

The pirates had already succeeded in disabling all of Prosper's turret batteries, and according to the distress signal Thatcher had received shortly after entering the system, they'd also boarded the station and taken hostages.

His course adjustments were designed to bring his formation straight to the pirate vessel that was most isolated from the other two. Based on their behavior, it seemed likely that word had managed to reach them about the *Jersey*'s lopsided engagement in the Olent Region, when those pirates had paid dearly for keeping their ships too close together. But these pirates had absorbed the lesson too well, keeping their ships as far apart from each other as possible. If they kept doing that, Thatcher would pick them apart with ease.

"We're less than a minute from entering effective firing range, sir," Lucy Guerrero said.

Thatcher nodded. Then, he saw it. The other two pirate ships had shifted their trajectories and were now angling around the station toward the lone vessel Thatcher intended to target. *So they're not totally clueless after all.* "Helm, increase engines to seventy percent. Ops, tell the *Squall* do the same, and send a directional jamming burst at the pirate vessel nearest us. *Victorious* and *Lightfoot* should hang back and prepare to engage the other enemy craft as needed. Tell Major Hancock to stand by to launch with Attack Shuttle One."

As he studied the unfolding engagement, Thatcher saw that his speed increase might not be sufficient. The other two pirate vessels had reacted quickly enough that they would have viable firing solutions on the *New Jersey*'s attack shuttle as it crossed to the station. Getting the marines aboard Prosper had been the true aim in isolating one of the enemy ships; knocking it off the board would merely have been a bonus.

"XO, launch a Hellborn at the rightmost enemy vessel. Tell the *Victorious* to send one at the leftmost, Ops." That should serve to occupy them while Attack Shuttle One slipped past the nearest enemy's blinded sensors.

Both rockets sprang forth, and the *Jersey*'s target reacted by putting up a shield, which the ordnance ruptured against almost harmlessly. The *Victorious'* target apparently had no shields, and it reversed course while attempting to swat the missile down with railguns.

Thatcher frowned. He'd been hoping *neither* ship would have shields. But the time had arrived.

"Tell Major Hancock to launch, Ops."

"Aye."

Next came the telltale shudder as Attack Shuttle One left its launch catapult with enough energy to cross the intervening void quickly. *But it'll still be vulnerable to that shielded ship.* To protect his marines, Thatcher would have to position the *Jersey* between that ship and the blinded one.

Except, the blinded vessel wouldn't remain so for much longer. It would already be working on electronic countermeasures to overcome the jamming, either hopping energy frequencies or using an omnidirectional antenna to eliminate the noise from their sensors. It might also receive sensor data from the other enemy ships. Once it got its bearings, it would eagerly move to sandwich the *Jersey*.

There's nothing for it. "Nav, set a course that interposes us between our shuttle's course and the shielded ship. I need a firing solution for that same ship, XO. Prepare to raise shields on my mark."

"Aye, Captain," said both Sullivan and Candle.

"Tell the *Lightfoot* we'll soon need some help keeping our shields up, Ops."

"Aye, sir."

"I have the firing solution, sir," Candle said. "Primary laser is armed and ready."

Thatcher glanced at the tactical display, which showed Attack Shuttle One sailing ever closer to the station. "Fire."

The *New Jersey*'s primary laser lanced out, hammering the pirates' force field and sending ripples of energy throughout it.

A moment later, the ship behind the *Jersey* apparently shrugged off the *Lightfoot*'s jamming. It began peppering the cruiser's shield, and the shielded pirate ship added its own laserfire.

"Shield power dropping sharply, sir," Guerrero said. "We're at seventy-three percent."

Thatcher felt his jaw tighten, and when he glanced at the tactical display, he saw that the third pirate ship had dealt with the Hellborn and was returning to join the fray.

"Sixty-two percent shield power," Guerrero said, just a few seconds later. Then: "The *Lightfoot* has begun maser energy transfer. Shields still dropping, but slower now. Fifty-nine percent."

Thatcher fought to keep his voice level. "Very good." His eyes were glued to the visual display on the upper-left corner of his holoscreen, where the *Jersey*'s primary laser continued to dump energy into the pirate craft's shield. He called up his own shield's power on the top-right of the screen—it had dipped to fifty-six percent. Certainly a slower drop, now that the logistics ship was feeding power to her receiver array via microwave beam. But when the third ship added its firepower...

She did so now, sending twin streams of solid-core rounds into the *New Jersey*.

"Forty-eight percent shield power and dropping fast once again, Captain," Guerrero said. Her words were redundant to Thatcher, now that he'd called up the percentage on his own holoscreen, but she was only following protocol. And it was important for the rest of the CIC crew to know the peril they were in.

Victorious added her own primary laser to *Jersey*'s, but still the pirate shield held fast. *It should be down by now.* Then, it struck him: *The station. They must be feeding power to her from the station.*

"Thirty-three percent, sir."

"Candle, have the forward gunners add their laserfire."

His XO twisted in his chair to peer at him. "Sir, the capacitor's already overtaxed with powering the primary as well as our—"

"It can handle it, with the power feed from the *Lightfoot*. Do it now."

The forward gunner crews began pelting the enemy shield with the *Jersey*'s secondaries, and a few seconds later it finally went down.

"Put a Hellborn in her, XO."

"Aye, sir."

"Ops, have Engineering prepare to deploy repair drones."

As the missile's departure sent a tremor through the cruiser's frame, her own shields reached zero, the force field dissipating under enemy fire. Neither the *Victorious* nor the *Jersey* flinched, however, and they continued to focus on destroying the pirate ship whose shields had also fallen.

The *Lightfoot* had already released a cloud of remote repair drones, which had almost reached Thatcher's ship to land on her hull and lend their efforts to the *Jersey*'s own drones.

At last the Hellborn reached its target, planting itself inside a section already melted by laserfire. The enemy vessel blew apart, and a ragged cheer rose up in the CIC.

"Bring us about, Nav, and take us away from the station on a course perpendicular to the enemy ships' turrets."

"Aye, sir."

The *Jersey*'s hull was taking extensive damage from the remaining enemies' railgun turrets, but increasing her transverse velocity relative to those turrets offered some protection, making it harder to track and hit her. Between that and the efforts of two repair drone complements, the beating was limited to just superficial damage.

The battle was all but over, and together with the *Victorious*, they neutralized a second enemy ship just four minutes later.

Such is the nature of warfare in space. It takes hours to maneuver into position, and minutes for engagements to play out.

Instead of destroying the third enemy ship outright, they managed to secure her surrender. Her hull was largely intact, and as Thatcher told Veronica Rose, "We can put her to good use. This isn't over. Guerrero detected a ship leaving the system just after the battle—we're pretty sure it saw everything. Our enemies will learn of what happened here soon enough."

"Do you expect Reardon to come at us?" she asked.

"Not Reardon. Not yet. First, they'll try to handle us without revealing their affiliation with pirates to the entire Cluster."

"So they'll send more of them at us, then."

Thatcher nodded. "I think we can expect everything within two hops of this system to come at us before the day's out."

CHAPTER TWENTY

On Prosper Station
Epact System, Dupliss Region
Earth Year 2290

CAPTAIN WILL AVERY CRAWLED ALONG THE LIFE SUPPORT service duct as quickly and quietly as he could, pushing his Dragon Tac-50 semi-automatic sniper rifle along ahead of him.

"Your ships are getting blown apart as we speak," Major Hancock, commander of the *Jersey*'s marine company, whispered into his ear—a whisper, since Avery's directional speaker was turned down as low as it would go. "We're your only way out of here. I repeat: do not harm any of those people. We're willing to negotiate with, but those people's lives are nonnegotiable."

"Everything is negotiable," a pirate answered back. "Particularly their lives, since we hold them in our hands. As it happens, I don't trust you. I don't think you have the firepower to destroy all three of our ships."

"Not all three?" Hancock shot back. "Just how many do you

think we'll destroy, then? Two? Two-and-a-half? Don't dick me about. I think you understand full well the position you're in."

Avery reached an intersection, where he could either continue straight or turn right. He consulted his eyepiece, which displayed a map of the service duct network he'd entered just a few minutes after Attack Shuttle One had docked with Prosper Station. He'd left his helmet behind—even though it was capable of syncing with his rifle's scope, he preferred to go natural.

"No pressure, Avery," Hancock had whispered as he'd pushed himself along that first stretch of cramped tunnel. "But you're those people's only hope for survival. We have time to play just one card before we need to clear the rest of the station. Else, the pirates will regroup and punish us for being so soft-hearted."

The hostages were being held inside a long, low control room that overlooked two repair bays as well as the docking bay where the marines had come in. Other than the bulkhead facing the station, the control room was surrounded by deck-to-overhead windows of bulletproof acrylic. The pirates stood in full view of the marines in the docking bay below, weapons pressed theatrically against their captives' heads. It would have been a simple matter for Hancock and his marines to rush the control room up the metal staircase that switched back and forth until it reached a standard-sized hatch, which Hancock would have ordered blown open. In that scenario, Avery would have stayed on the docking bay deck, to shoot any pirates who tried to use the high ground against the ascending marines. With the Frontier marines' training and silver power armor, Avery wouldn't be surprised if they mowed down every last pirate in there without taking any casualties. But the hostages would never have made it.

So Avery had begun his journey through the duct system, climbing ladders and squeezing himself through spaces that would make most men feel claustrophobic. Hell, it made him feel a little cramped, if he was being honest.

Six pirates. At least, six we could see through the window. Luckily, his weapon was self-loading, and the distance between the grate he intended to use as his hide and the acrylic window was no more than seventy-five meters. Accuracy shouldn't be a problem, and neither would having to pause to reload. *Shooting them before they can react might be.*

He was banking on their shock being enough to throw them off without causing them to take it out on the hostages. What these pirates apparently didn't realize was that Frontier had been given detailed schematics for every station and Helio base in Dupliss, as part of the Oasis contract. *I guess Pegg considered it too big a risk to share that intel with them. If the pirates were found to have it, then the cat would be out of the bag about them colluding.*

The way Avery saw it, if you were going to be a scumbag, you might as well commit to it. Now these pirates would pay for Pegg's waffling.

"We want a shuttle out of here," said the same pirate as before. Hancock had continued to wear him down as Avery crawled through the ducts, just as the major wore his marines down during daily PT. *And I don't mean physically. The way that man gets inside your head...*

"And safe passage out of the system," the pirate continued. "We'll take the hostages with us, and we'll dump them in their suits near the jump gate. You can come and collect them five hours after we're gone—their suits will keep them alive for up to eight, yes?"

"That's right," Hancock mused. "But tell me something. How do we know you'll keep up your end of the bargain?"

"You don't," the pirate said. "But this is your only chance to save these people."

Avery finally reached the grate and immediately detached the laser cutter from his belt, switched it to a low-power setting, and started in. The cutter gave a low whine as he ran it along the grate's edges, and its muzzle flashed, but it shouldn't be enough to alert the pirates. He prayed it wouldn't, anyway.

Just before he finished detaching the grate, he fished for his magnetic gripper and pressed it against the grate, turning it on. Then he finished his cutting, and the grate came free of its casing. He pushed it out beyond the duct a little, turned it horizontal, and slid it underneath him. All as silently as possible.

Hancock was still conducting his phony negotiation with the pirates, none of whom had noticed Avery at work, seventy-five meters behind them. He crawled back a foot and set up his Dragon at the duct's mouth, extending the telescoping bipod to rest against the metal floor. Then he stuffed in a set of earplugs.

Before shooting, he eyeballed his six targets, all lined up nicely with their backs to him. He sequenced them in his head as they stood arrogantly before the acrylic glass, sure they were safe from the marines below.

And you are. Safe from those *marines, anyway.*

He peered through the scope and sucked in a breath, then let it out in a slow exhale. His body lay perfectly still, and his fingers did not shake.

The shot boomed in the narrow duct, deafening even through the earplugs. His first target's head exploded, blood and bone spattering the hostage he'd been threatening.

Avery shifted the barrel smoothly to the next pirate, who was turning. The round took him in the neck, ripping in and out, and the man staggered back to entangle himself with the hostage he'd been responsible for.

He nudged the rifle a couple centimeters to the right. Now the pirates were lifting their weapons as their eyes roved wildly around the long control room, looking for who was shooting at them, terror on their faces. *I need to shoot faster.* His next round blew a pirate's shoulder apart, and he gut-shot the fourth target.

But the rightmost pirate was gaining his bearings. He grabbed his hostage, a male not long out of adolescence, and swung him around, lodging the muzzle of his assault rifle under his chin. "Stop!" Avery recognized the voice as the same one that had been negotiating with Hancock. "Stop shooting!"

But Avery didn't stop. He couldn't. He blew apart his fifth target's jaw, and he took careful aim at the last pirate standing, tracking his erratic movements and taking another breath.

Then it happened: the pirate pulled the trigger, sending several rounds into the boy's skull. Avery shot him a second later, but it was too late.

"Damn it," he yelled. "God damn it all!"

"Easy, Avery," Hancock said. "Keep it together. You saved five people. That's good work."

"I should have made the shot quicker. I could have saved them all, Major."

"Avery, calm down. That's an order."

"Yes, Major." The pirate he'd shot in the shoulder was struggling toward his weapon, so Avery blew off the top of his head. Next, he put down the one he'd gut-shot.

With that, he safetied his weapon, retracted the bipod, and placed the weapon on the duct floor, so as not to spook the surviving former hostages any more than they already had been. That done, he lowered his forehead to the cool metal of the grate and continued to berate himself mentally.

"I'm sorry, Avery," Hancock said. "Taking this station is going to cost us, that much is clear. The worst thing is, I'm beginning to believe the captain doesn't intend to reward us for our efforts."

For a few seconds, Avery didn't answer. "Are we on a private channel right now, Major?"

"Of course."

"You don't think he's going to start cutting the marines in on prize money?"

"I'm not sure he intends to distribute any prize money, to anyone. He thinks he's back in the Fleet, where he can send people hopping at a word, no questions asked. But we both know things have always been a bit looser than that, on the *Jersey*. A lot of us got into this gig hoping to make some extra coin, didn't we?"

"Well, there's not much we can do about it, Major," Avery said, his forehead still firmly against the metal.

"Oh, I think there is. I think it's time we *demand* our fair share."

CHAPTER TWENTY-ONE

Aboard Attack Shuttle One
Epact System, Dupliss Region
Earth Year 2290

MOST OF THE MARINE PLATOON RIDING ON ATTACK SHUTTLE One had taken off their helmets and stowed them under their crash seats, to get a bit of fresh air before donning them again to board the *Charger*, the pirate corvette that had surrendered to Captain Thatcher.

As fresh as you can get in space, anyway.

Avery kept his helmet on, and so did Major Hancock, as well as Lieutenant Commander Billy Candle—*New Jersey*'s XO. This way, they could converse in secret.

"Things are changing in the Cluster," Hancock was saying. "There's no need to abide captains who think they can get everything from those under their command for nothing in return. Not anymore."

Without turning his head, Avery watched the XO as he seemed to weigh Hancock's words from his crash seat across the aisle. None of them moved as they spoke, instead staring straight ahead and remaining perfectly motionless. The helmets were enough of a giveaway that they were having a secret conversation, though a few other marines had left theirs on, thankfully. Possibly for the same reason.

Taking Prosper Station had been about as agonizing as expected. Hancock had made good use of Avery, sending him throughout the station's nooks and crannies to get the drop on clusters of hostiles. The pirates were woefully outmatched, wielding unintegrated weapons, with their patchwork armor pitted against the marines' silver power suits.

Even so, there'd been three marine casualties, one of them critical. Avery thought Underwood would make it—he was a tough son of a bitch—but he wouldn't be sent back into battle for a while.

To top it all off, two more hostages had died as they retook the station. Neither of those was Avery's fault, but he couldn't stop his mind from playing and replaying the scene from the control room. The way he'd fumbled that last shot…

If I'd just been a little faster.

Thatcher had been about to send Attack Shuttle Two to secure the *Charger*, but Hancock had insisted Alpha Platoon was up for the job, even after slogging through Prosper Station. "We're suited up already, sir, more than warmed up, and in no mood to take any shit from pirates, if you'll pardon me. It's just as well to send us."

Unknown to the captain, the marine commander had patched Avery into the exchange. He'd listened and stayed silent.

"Very well, Major," Thatcher had said, clearly ready to defer to Hancock's judgment. That had killed Avery, a little—everyone said Thatcher was an obsessive micromanager, yet here he was trusting his marine commander to handle things. The same marine commander who planned to betray him.

So they'd dropped off the casualties at the *Jersey* and taken on the XO, as well as a couple other officers Thatcher had delegated to operate the *Charger* in the coming battle. Some more crew were being sent over in Attack Shuttle Two—as many as would be needed to oversee the pirate crew and make sure they did exactly as they were ordered, backed up by marine muscle.

"Just what are you proposing?" Candle said at last.

"Well, that depends on you, sir," Hancock said. For the record, I'm not proposing anything until you say you're in. But I know you miss the way things were under Captain Vaughn."

"I don't think things will ever be that way again on the *Jersey*."

"Not on the *Jersey*, no. Maybe not on any Frontier ship. But we have to start thinking outside the box, don't we? Like I said, things are different now. For instance, if a PMC employee were to skip out on the rest of his contract, who would have the time or resources to stop him? Especially if that employee, or employees, had a fully operational corvette at their disposal to use as a big fat bargaining chip. We could work for any corp we want. Or we could explore...*other* endeavors."

Hancock had been Avery's friend since they'd endured Fleet boot camp together, years and years ago. But Hancock's ambition had seen him get promoted a little faster than his friend, and when his second enlistment date rolled around, he quit the Fleet to work for Frontier, while Avery stuck around for another term.

Nearly eight years later, when they'd reconnected on Earth, Hancock had talked him into applying for a job with Frontier, offering to put in a good word for him. It had worked out, and once aboard the *Jersey*, they'd found their friendship just as fresh as it had always been. It made Avery a bit uncomfortable, since Hancock was now his direct superior, but the marine commander insisted things were different here than they were in the Fleet.

So it was natural that Hancock would unquestioningly involve Avery in any secret plan to undermine the captain's authority.

Except, Avery didn't want to go against Thatcher. Yes, the whispered talk against the captain was plentiful—on the mess decks, in the ship's quiet spots, and even in the engine room, or so Avery had heard. There was always talk about what a hardass Thatcher was, or about the lack of prize money. But Avery had noticed that it was always the same people complaining, and their listeners often made only noncommittal sounds, and wore carefully guarded expressions.

There's enough talk to make you think everyone hates the captain. But I respect him. And I bet a lot of others do, too. They're just afraid to say it, for fear of being outcast.

He didn't want to undermine Thatcher, or mutiny, or defect, or whatever it was Hancock had in mind. But the XO actually seemed to be considering it. And if the *XO* would go against Thatcher...what hope was there? For him, or for Frontier Security in its current form?

Avery had a family back on Mars—a wife and twin sons—and he wanted to get back to them. He woke every morning now to the thought of the Xanthic infiltrating the enclosed colony where they lived, and he wanted nothing more than to protect them, to fight the yellow bugs back into whatever hole they came from.

He couldn't do that by defecting, or mutinying. In fact, he saw Captain Thatcher as his way back to Sol System, if a way even existed. Because everyone knew the captain wanted the same thing.

Then again, if the marines on this shuttle turned against Thatcher, against Frontier—what could Avery do? If he died opposing them, he definitely wouldn't get back to Sarah and the boys.

"I'm with you," the XO said, and Avery's heart sank. "Now tell me what you're planning."

CHAPTER TWENTY-TWO

Aboard the *New Jersey*
Epact System, Dupliss Region
Earth Year 2290

"Who is it?" Thatcher asked, his thumb on the intercom button while his eyes remained glued to the holoscreen, where he'd been shuffling ship icons around the Epact System in an attempt to foresee how the coming engagement would likely unfold.

"I am Hans Mittelman," said a voice with a slight German accent. "Ms. Rose asked me to come speak with you."

Thatcher sniffed sharply, staring at the closed hatch. He was loathe to waste time he could be using to plan on chitchat. "What's your position with Frontier?"

"It wouldn't be wise to say so while standing in an open passageway, with your crew scurrying to and fro."

Frowning, Thatcher tapped the button to unlock the hatch. "Come in."

The hatch swung open to reveal a man who looked about as old as Thatcher but had already gone completely gray, except for the shaggy patch of hair beneath his lower lip, which was still dark. He stepped over the lip of the hatch with a primness that matched his crisp, patterned black-and-gray blazer.

Closing the hatch, he turned to fold his hands before him, the corners of his mouth curving as he studied Thatcher with sharp, storm-colored eyes. "May I sit, Commander?"

Thatcher gave a curt nod.

"You'll forgive me for not observing the proper military protocol I know you're so fond of," Mittelman said, lowering himself to the chair in front of Thatcher's desk and crossing one leg over the other. "Technically I would outrank you, if I had a rank. But like Ms. Rose, I do not. Either way, I won't make you salute me."

"What's your position with Frontier?"

"Chief Intelligence Officer. Spymaster, you might as well call me, since officially no one knows Frontier even *has* a CIO. The savvy ones probably suspect we do, but I'm completely off the books. Works out well, come tax time."

Thatcher raised an eyebrow, unsure if that was a joke or not.

"Suffice it to say I know what goes on aboard the *New Jersey* better than you do, especially now that young Ensign Devine blew his own cover."

Now how do you know that? Thatcher himself had only learned about Devine's outburst a couple of hours ago. But he didn't intend to give Mittelman the satisfaction of asking, or to provide him with the reaction he so clearly wanted. "Why are you here?"

"I've obtained some information which seems important to your success as captain of the *New Jersey*. I alerted Ms. Rose to this information, and she instructed me to approach you, not only to offer the information, but also to offer you the full extent of my services. She barely trusts anyone with the knowledge of my existence, so you should take my presence as a profound compliment. You must be an impressive man indeed, to have earned her esteem."

Thatcher shrugged, unwilling to buy into the flattery.

A fleeting frown passed across Mittelman's face—a slight bunching of the brow, a twitch of the mouth. An inattentive observer would have missed the microexpression. *He's probing me. Searching for the levers that will let him manipulate me. Will he find them?*

"Of course, if you consider yourself too *honorable* to avail of a spymaster's services, that's your business." Mittelman spoke just as smoothly as before, though with a certain flatness. "However, I strongly believe that to spurn my gifts would prove to your detriment."

"Is that so," Thatcher said mildly. "Well, in my view, it wouldn't be honorable to ignore a weapon available for use against an enemy. It would be stupid."

Mittelman nodded, and though his smile didn't return, Thatcher sensed a renewed gravity in his next words. "Then I believe we will accomplish great things together, Commander. The information I have for you pertains to the situation aboard the *Charger*, your new pirate prize. There's a high probability that situation will turn mutinous, with your XO and marine commander as key players."

"How do you know that?"

"I intercepted their communications, of course."

"How?"

Mittelman smiled, when Thatcher would have expected annoyance. *Either he has excellent control of himself, or his is an alien mind indeed.*

"It wouldn't be wise for me to share my methods with you, Captain, for many reasons. One being OPSEC. The more people I tell about the techniques I use, the more likely it becomes that defenses will be developed against them. Another reason is that you will likely judge my methods unsavory."

And a third reason: he's almost certainly using those same methods on me.

Maybe Mittelman had a sense of Thatcher's train of thought, since he quickly spoke again. "I should stress just how vital operational security is for my work. You yourself recognized the issue when you refused to share your battle plan with your officers."

Mittelman hadn't been flying with the *Jersey* and the *Squall* then—clearly, he had other methods of intelligence gathering than mere communications interception. Much older methods, if Thatcher were to guess.

"The fact is," the CIO went on, "the Dawn Cluster is a fluid environment, and individuals can enjoy handsome rewards by providing information to those who should not have it. Spies have been a problem since the first corporations began operating here, but now that the wormhole has closed and tensions are rising, I can virtually guarantee the problem will get ten times worse."

"Giving you fantastic job security."

"Indeed."

Thatcher nodded. "Well, I appreciate you coming to me. As for the situation aboard the *Charger*, I intend to do nothing. I sensed the major was capable of treachery the moment I met him, but the jury's out on Candle. And so, it's time to give him enough rope to hang himself. If he turns on us, it will be at the worst possible time, I'm sure—but I am prepared for the eventuality."

CHAPTER TWENTY-THREE

Aboard the *Sabre*
Epact System, Dupliss Region
Earth Year 2290

THE FAMILIAR LURCH OF SYSTEM JUMPING, AND THEN THE *SABRE* arrived in Epact.

"Active sensor sweeps right away, Earl," said the frigate's captain, a long-time buccaneer named Cassandra Beitler. "Tell me what you see."

"Yes, ma'am," her sensor operator said, peering at his display. "The other five ships successfully made the jump as well."

"Very good." She'd know more once data started coming in from the active sweeps. They would trumpet their arrival to the entire system, but she felt sure that this Thatcher was closely monitoring every system jump zone anyway. *He's not to be underestimated.* At least, not based on what her new business partners told her.

A tiny thrill shot through her at that phrase: *business partners.* It spoke of the new opportunities emerging on the Dawn

Cluster's periphery, opportunities she never thought she would live to see. For decades, it had always been her and her crew, a tight-knit bunch she considered something close to family. Preying on unaccompanied mining vessels, raiding small outposts—this was their bread and butter. But now, they all shared in the excitement of something bigger. Something grander.

A pirate corp. Could it really be possible? She thought about it every day, and she still couldn't see a reason why not.

The *Sabre*'s crew would be perfect for such an organization, she knew. Yes, they shared strong bonds, but they were also professional, in defiance of the stereotypes most people held about pirates. She'd never venture to call what they did respectable work, but they did it well. And she knew plenty of other captains whose crews were almost as effective. *Yes. This can work.*

But I need to focus on the matter at hand. She forced herself out of her daydreaming, her gaze landing on Earl Van de Hey, once more, who was hunched over his console, squinting at it fiercely.

"What do you see, Earl?"

"It's the *Charger*, ma'am. She's approaching our formation."

She cocked her head sideways. "Donnie Middleton's ship? I thought she was destroyed."

"Apparently not. They left her intact, for whatever reason. She's alone. Of the Frontier and Sunder vessels, I'm seeing the light cruiser and destroyer orbiting near Prosper Station, but no sign of their electronic warfare or logistics ships."

"The *Charger*'s hailing us, ma'am," her coms operator said.

I don't trust any of this. "Put it through."

A man with ebony skin and bright green eyes appeared on the bridge's main display. "Greetings."

"Who are you? And where's Captain Middleton?"

"I'm Lieutenant Commander Billy Candle, with Frontier

Security. Mr. Middleton surrendered to my CO, Commander Thatcher. He's still aboard the *Charger*, but as a prisoner."

"Then prepare to be fired on," Beitler said, her voice cold. Just as she saw her crew as family, she considered the captains the *Sabre* shared hot-zone space with to be extended family. Other than the occasional pirate-on-pirate raid, of course...but she only did that to commanders she disliked.

"Just a second," Candle said. "I think you'll find it advantageous to *not* fire on us."

"How do you figure that?"

"Do you think my orders were to come and reveal myself to you immediately? Wouldn't it have been much smarter to hold Captain Middleton at gunpoint and force him to tell you that all is well aboard the *Charger*?"

Beitler drummed her fingers once on her chair's armrest. "Do you mean to try convincing me that you're going against your captain?"

"I do. Because I am. *We* are: I also have the *New Jersey*'s marine commander here with me, along with half the marine company, and they're all of the same mind. Captain Thatcher's been a disappointment to us, and with the Cluster changing like it is, we plan to look to other horizons to make our fortunes."

"What horizons?"

Candle shrugged. "I know you probably won't admit to working with Reardon Interstellar, but everyone knows you are. If you ask me, Reardon should just come out and admit it—though I guess they want plausible deniability, in case the wormhole reopens. Anyway, that doesn't matter. I don't think the wormhole is going to open, and I never joined Frontier for the sort of 'good cause' that seems to drive Thatcher. I joined to make money. If the company's getting away from that, then I want to join up with a corp that has its shit together. The UNC's sitting in the middle of the Cluster with its hands tied, which means there's a killing to be made for corps that move fast enough. If you're forming a corp, I want in, and so do the marines here. Of course, we'll want our fair share of any spoils from the battle we're about to help you win."

Beitler studied Candle's face. "You're asking for a lot of trust based on very little."

The Frontier officer spread his hands. "What can I do to convince you I'm being honest?"

"You're *not* being honest, for one. You're betraying your captain—that's not honest. But I can definitely work with it, if I'm persuaded that betrayal is genuine. Here's what you can do to persuade me. I want intel. And a lot of it."

CHAPTER TWENTY-FOUR

Aboard the *Sabre*
Epact System, Dupliss Region
Earth Year 2290

"IF REARDON STILL WANTS TO MAINTAIN DENIABILITY," CANDLE said from her console display as all seven ships crossed the Epact System together, "then we should probably take out the *Jersey* and the *Victorious* and then salvage the scrap from their wrecks. Nothing has to get out about pirates doing Reardon's dirty work for them. And as an added bonus, Frontier and Sunder will both lose their CEOs, along with a bunch of execs, in Frontier's case. Ramon Pegg will be happy about that."

"I still haven't said we're working with Reardon," Beitler said, and Candle just rolled his eyes. That made her smile in spite of herself. "How many missiles does each ship carry?"

She'd taken Candle off the bridge's main screen and replaced his image there with a tactical display, so that her officers could focus on the coming engagement. In the meantime, she busied herself with extracting all the information she could before reaching the moon Prosper Station orbited. "I don't know about the *Victorious*," Candle said, "but the *Jersey* has nearly its full complement of Hellborns, less the four we've fired since we last restocked in the Clime Region. So, forty-six."

"Her other weapons are fully operational, I presume?"

"I'm afraid so. Her automated railgun turrets are online, and so is her primary laser—although without me on board, Thatcher will have to rely on Tim Ortega to operate the primary, and he isn't as good a shot. The secondary lasers are all in working order as well, and the *Jersey*'s gunner crews are among the best in the Cluster. You may have six ships at your disposal, Captain—seven, counting the *Charger*—but it wouldn't be smart to count Thatcher out yet. I watched him outmaneuver seven ships in Olent, and neutralize all of them with just the *Jersey* and the *Squall*."

"We're ten minutes from entering effective firing range on the targets, ma'am," Earl Van de Hey said.

"Acknowledged." She turned back to Candle. "The *Squall* is an electronic warfare ship, correct?

"Yes."

"Where is she now?"

"She was destroyed in the engagement near Prosper Station, along with the Sunder logistics vessel, the *Lightfoot*."

"Very good. I heard Thatcher's victory in Olent hinged on tricks he played using his eWar ship, so I'm glad to hear it's gone."

Candle nodded. "Exactly."

Beitler was watching the Frontier officer closely. "I also heard he did something fancy with his missiles. Something unheard of. Were you planing to mention that, Commander?"

"It didn't seem necessary, since that maneuver required extensive jamming to pull off—something Thatcher couldn't execute now even if he had the *Squall*, with the way you've spread out your ships. I don't want to waste our time discussing tactics not relevant to the immediate engagement."

"Right." She leaned back in her chair a little, considering the tactical display on the bridge's main screen. "Under normal circumstances, I'd order all ships to target down the destroyer first. But you've made me consider that focusing our fire on Thatcher's light cruiser might be the best move, here."

"It likely is, Captain."

She hadn't yet told Candle her name, so he'd resorted to calling her "captain." If they both got through this engagement intact, she intended to change that. Candle had a certain charm about him, and though he had to be at least fifteen years her junior, she'd begun to wonder if a dinner with him in her quarters might be arranged. *I can help you rise far in the corp we're building. If you play your cards right.* The thought surprised her, but it also curled the corners of her lips. *My, my.*

Earl Van de Hey went rigid at his console again. "Ma'am." For a moment, he didn't continue. His gaze flitted to her console, then to her face. "Can I have a word?"

Instantly, she knew something was wrong. "Just say it, Earl."

"I've been analyzing the debris around Prosper Station. There's no way four vessels were destroyed there, as our new *friend* is claiming. It can't have been any more than two ships. The ones Thatcher and his people destroyed themselves."

Beitler turned back to her console's screen and attempted to burn a hole through Candle's skull with her gaze. "You have ten seconds to explain the meaning of this."

"Only two ships?" Candle wore a blank expression. "That doesn't make any sense. You must be missing some sensor data. Here, I'll be back in a moment."

"Wait. Missing sensor data?" Beitler narrowed her eyes. "That's impossible. We've been running active scans ever since we arrived in—"

But the display had gone blank. Candle had cut off their conversation.

SCOTT BARTLETT

"The *Charger* just launched an Ogre at us," Van de Hey shouted. "Her batteries are firing on us as well!"

Then came the rumble of solid-core rounds hitting her ship.

"You bastard," she spat, meaning Candle, though Van de Hey shot her a scandalized look. "Tactical, fire back with everything we have!"

146

CHAPTER TWENTY-FIVE

Aboard the *New Jersey*
Epact System, Dupliss Region
Earth Year 2290

"They sniffed out the *Charger* early, Captain," Lucy Guerrero said, barely able to push the words out. "They're firing on her."

Damn. A few more minutes would have put the pirates right where he wanted them. So much of warfare was appearing weaker than you really were, so the enemy would attack you where you wanted them to.

I can still work with this. But it's going to be a slugfest, now. "Engines full ahead, Helm, and Guerrero, have the *Victorious* join the charge. Tell the support ships to come out from behind that moon. I want the *Squall* to jam as many of the ships firing on the *Charger* as she can."

"Just to confirm, sir—not omnidirectional jamming, then?"

"Correct. Directional only. We certainly aren't running from this, and we can't afford to blind ourselves."

Cruiser and destroyer raced across the intervening void, mere minutes from entering effective firing range. In the meantime, Candle was taking a beating in the *Charger*. The corvette had no shields, and though its small complement of repair drones buzzed across her hull, welding rifts shut here and replacing sections there as the ship fled at full power, their efforts were already being overtaken by the sheer firepower the pirates were bringing to bear.

Did this mean Candle was loyal after all, or merely that he intended to wait until after the engagement to move against Thatcher? He couldn't tell, but it did come as a relief that the *Charger* hadn't joined the pirates in fighting him. He wouldn't have wanted to destroy a ship with several of his officers and half his marines aboard it.

"Ortega, calculate a firing solution for the corvette I'm designating." He tapped the icon representing the target, and the vessel flashed red inside the holotank at the CIC's fore, just as it would on his Chief Tactical Officer's display. "Let's open with a Hellborn and follow with laserfire from our forward gunners. Send your targeting data to Guerrero, for sharing with the *Victorious*."

"Aye, sir."

Mittelman had again made himself useful soon after their initial meeting, by providing intelligence on three of the six pirate ships that had appeared in Epact. The corvette Thatcher had designated was one of them, and according to the spymaster's profile, it lacked shields. It also sat in the dead center of the pirate formation, close enough to pressure the *Charger* but too far for the *Squall* to jam her. Neutralizing that corvette would go a long way to securing his people's safety.

"I have the firing solution, Captain," Ortega said. "Ready to fire on your command."

"Fire."

The *Jersey* shuddered with the Hellborn's departure, and moments later the *Squall* rounded the moon's horizon, popping onto the tactical display. She was followed almost immediately by the *Lightfoot*.

Excellent. "Have our logistics ship make for the *Charger* with all haste, Guerrero, to add her repair drones to the corvette's."

The eWar ship would have begun jamming the two nearest pirate vessels—both frigates—the moment she had line of sight, and soon Thatcher saw the effects of that interference: those ships began shooting wild, their fire tapering as they tried to fight off the jamming.

In the meantime, the *Jersey*'s Hellborn struck home, slamming into her target's hull and blasting her open wide enough that it would take repair drones ten minutes or more to mend the fissure.

Thatcher's eyes locked onto the back of his tactical officer's head. "The forward gunners will direct their fire into that spot."

"Aye, sir."

Blue laserfire shot across the battlespace from multiple batteries, and a pair of Hellborns from the *Victorious* closed in to finish the job. The targeted corvette ruptured all along her hull, expelling equipment and crew into the breathless void.

The *Lightfoot*'s first repair drones landed on the *Charger*, which was finally putting meaningful distance between it and its pursuers. The three remaining unjammed pirate vessels now turned their attention on the ships that had just dismantled one of their own.

"Reverse thrust, Helm. Guerrero, signal to the *Victorious* to do the same."

"Aye, sir," came the reply from both officers.

The jammed frigates would be clearing their sensors about now, no doubt with the help of sensor feeds from their allied ships. That left the enemy captains with a choice: continue chasing the *Charger*, make for the *Squall*, or join their allies in chasing down Captains Thatcher and Moll.

He decided he would make the choice for them. "Ortega, target the *Sabre* with our primary laser." Unlike the corvette they'd destroyed, Thatcher knew this ship to have shields. He lacked any intel about the other frigate, but it was of a similar make, and he felt safe assuming it also had them. Currently, neither vessel had shields raised, but by leading with his primary he gave himself the chance of melting part of the *Sabre*'s hull, while still having a meaningful effect if she raised her shields, since lasers worked best for taking those down.

The Sunder destroyer quickly added her own primary to *Jersey*'s, and while they connected only briefly with the frigate's exposed hull, once she raised her shields they began to shimmer spastically under the strain.

All five pirate ships were giving chase, now. The frigates loosed a missile each, then followed with lasers of their own, while the remaining corvette fired railguns, as did the two converted freighters. Every shot had been aimed at the *New Jersey* as she continued to fall back.

"Shields up," Thatcher said.

"Aye, sir." Ortega tapped at his console. "Raising shields now."

The concentrated fire hammered the force field, causing it to ripple with even greater violence than the *Sabre*'s.

Guerrero gripped both sides of her console as she stared at the falling numbers, calling them out. "Down to seventy-four percent shield power, sir. Sixty-eight percent. Sixty-three."

But Thatcher's attention was on the holotank, where the 3D model representing the *New Jersey* inched backward, getting closer and closer to Prosper Station as the pirates continued to abuse her shield.

"Fifty-one percent." Guerrero's voice thrummed with tension. "Forty-four."

The shields fell all the way to thirty-two percent—and then his operations officer gave an audible sigh of relief. "The station has begun maser energy transfer, sir. Shield power is still dropping, but much slower now. Thirty-one percent."

At that moment, the *Sabre*'s shields gave way under the concentrated firepower of *Jersey*'s and *Victorious*'s primary lasers. The bright beams extended to connect with her hull once more, and though she reversed thrust immediately, trying to evade the lasers while her repair drones scurried toward the damage, it was too late. The energy being dumped into the *Sabre*'s frame tore her apart.

Thatcher allowed himself a small smile. The pirates from the last engagement, who'd used the station to bolster their own shields, had shown him a neat trick, and he wasn't above learning from his enemies. Far from it. *Your greatest enemy is your greatest teacher.* A Buddhist proverb, if he remembered correctly. He wondered what Ramon Pegg would have to teach him.

"Target the nearest converted freighter with our primary. And send a Hellborn their way for good measure. Guerrero, request that Captain Moll do the same." Now that the need to lure the frigates had passed, he could focus on wiping the smaller vessels from the battlespace. "Helm, full ahead thrust."

The pirates were in retreat, now, perhaps having realized why *Jersey* had pulled back to the station. *It's too late for you, I'm afraid.* He'd positioned a shield readout in the corner of his holo-screen, and he saw its health indicators were all creeping back up. Soon, his cruiser's receiver array would move out of the station's microwave beam range, and the numbers would start falling again. But he doubted they'd fall fast enough to matter.

The digital model representing the converted freighter vanished from the tactical display, leaving a shattered wreck in its place. With that, they shifted targets to the other one, which quickly fell.

Two pirate ships remained. Beyond them, Candle had brought the *Charger* back around, her hull in slightly better condition than before, with the double helping of repair drones working on her.

Thatcher almost chuckled at the textbook neatness of the savage flanking maneuver unfolding within the holotank. Minutes later, the engagement was over, without a single casualty taken.

"The *Charger*'s hailing us, sir." Guerrero's voice came out much steadier than before. "It's Commander Candle."

"Put him through."

Candle's face replaced the tactical display on the holotank—a 2D representation, since the corvette's bridge lacked the necessary sensors to render him in 3D.

"We have a situation over here, sir."

"What's going on?"

"Major Hancock's trying to take over the ship—has been ever since we turned against the pirates, which, uh, wasn't in the plan he thought I'd agreed to. I'm requesting that you send over some marines whose loyalty can be guaranteed. If you'd like, I can make some recommendations."

CHAPTER TWENTY-SIX

Aboard the *Charger*
Epact System, Dupliss Region
Earth Year 2290

CORPORAL EMMONS HAD TRIED HIS BEST TO TALK THATCHER OUT of boarding Attack Shuttle Two and heading over to the *Charger* with his marines, but he failed.

"Get me a suit of power armor," Thatcher had said flatly. He was willing to make that concession to his safety, but the chance of him remaining on the *Jersey*, of leaving his mutinying marines for Emmons and his men to deal with, was zero. This was his responsibility.

Emmons had returned his gaze with an anguished expression, but they both knew time was of the essence, and he could no doubt see the resolve in Thatcher's eyes. *This ends today. Either we leave this system with a crew united under my command, or we don't leave it at all.*

Now, he crossed the shuttle's airlock and stepped over the docking bay's threshold, his sidearm's holster unclasped and ready to be drawn. Emmons had already taken in a squad of marines to clear the *Charger*'s bay, and they'd given the green light for the captain to enter.

When he did, he strode toward the nearby control station connected to the loudspeakers located throughout the ship. Once there, he snatched up the mic and pressed the button to sync it up with his helmet.

"Marines of the *New Jersey*. I understand Major Hancock has taken it upon himself to make our day even more challenging than it already was. When your commander takes it upon himself to incite a mutiny against your captain while aboard a different vessel altogether, it puts you in a difficult position, and I want every one of you to know I understand that."

He gave his words a moment to sink in, knowing that Hancock had no way of interrupting him, or even responding. Currently, the man was overseeing four marines and five pirates as they used tools they'd removed from repair drones to cut through the armored citadel the bridge had become.

Candle had lowered the citadel's solid-core steel hatches moments before he'd broken step with Hancock's plan, and now he was patching two camera feeds through to Emmons' eyepiece: a view of the marine commander's efforts to break in, and another of the marines and pirates Hancock had assigned to guard the only elevator connecting this deck to the bridge. A few bulkheads and passageways were all that stood between that elevator and the docking bay.

"We have a delicate situation." Thatcher planted a left hand on the bulkhead near the control station, shifting his weight for comfort. "How do you respond when an irresponsible leader places such unreasonable demands on you? How can you tell the difference between those truly committed to mutiny and those merely playing along for fear they'd be killed if they did otherwise? You can't—not at first. You must play along too, at least until you get your bearings. It's what I would do, and it's what Lieutenant Commander Billy Candle did. He humored

Hancock, playing the part well enough that Hancock left the bridge to him, leaving him in a position to act. But even then, Commander Candle had to take a chance. Could he truly be sure the other officers in the bridge were among the good guys? He thought he knew them, but did he really? He had to gamble. And thanks to his bravery, his heroism, this mutiny will fail.

"I know that most of you are with me. That you're loyal to me, to the company that hired you…to the USA, and to humanity. I know you want to do your part in helping Frontier to build a strong Dawn Cluster, so that we can return to Earth Local Space in force and defeat the Xanthic once and for all. I won't try to entice you with prize money, with riches, because I know you come from better stock than that. You aren't mere mercenaries hired by some private military company. Frontier Security hires its marines directly *from* the marines—the U.S. Marine Corps. Once a marine, always a marine. And we all know a real marine can be counted on.

"But you still have to take a chance, just as Commander Candle did. A few of the men around you really have lost their way, and they will kill you if they can, the moment you show signs of doing the right thing. I'm not going to hide my intentions from you. First, I will take the marines I brought with me to secure the elevator. After that, I'll deal with Hancock. The rest is up to you, marines. Semper Fi."

He placed the mic on its cradle and turned to find the marines accompanying him all standing at attention, saluting him.

"Oorah!" they shouted as one.

Thatcher returned their salute, and an exterior helmet speaker delivered his reply. "Oorah!"

With that, they moved out from the docking bay, navigating using the schematics Candle had forwarded to their eyepieces. Though Thatcher hadn't worn power armor since his time in the academy, he found it akin to riding a bicycle: he quickly reaccustomed himself with the way the form-fitting suit amplified his every movement, roughly tripling his strength.

They came to the passageway before the one that led to the elevator, halting before turning the final corner. "How should we proceed, sir?" Emmons asked him.

Thatcher almost told him to use his own judgment, but stopped himself. This was a highly unusual situation, wasn't it? Typically, he would have recommended striking hard and fast to take a vessel from a hostile force. But here, that would run counter to his objective—to keep bloodshed to a minimum.

"Deploy into the next corridor as quickly and as orderly as you can, training your weapons on pirates, not marines. If we must shoot, we'll shoot them first, then take cover." The power armor's protection would buy them a few seconds to safely withdraw, if it became necessary.

"Yes, sir," Emmons said. "Marines, move out!"

They did as Thatcher had ordered, and he rounded the corner with them, pistol raised. As he'd hoped, there was no immediate gunfire. Instead, both forces stared at each other across the long passageway, for several dragged-out seconds. It wasn't difficult to tell marine from pirate: the latter's armor was a mismatched patchwork that left plenty of gaps for a marksman to exploit.

Then, one of the marines guarding the elevator barked a single order: "Marines, fall back!"

As one, the *New Jersey* marines at the end of the passageway drew back, forming up near the elevator and leaving the pirates exchanging confused glances, clearly uncertain how to react.

"Drop your weapons and put your hands in the air, scumbags!" the same marine barked. This time, Thatcher's eyepiece analyzed the voice and provided him with a rank and name: Captain Will Avery.

The pirates shifted even more, their weapons wavering.

"Yes, I mean you," Avery said. "You are surrounded by Frontier marines, and if you do not drop your weapons immediately we will shoot you dead."

Finally, they seemed to get the message. The pirates slowly crouched, laying their weapons on the deck, then stood with their hands raised.

That done, Emmons sent marines forward to collect the firearms, safetying them as they did. At the same time, Avery ordered some of his marines to press the pirates against the wall and search them.

When the pirates were all gathered together, Thatcher crossed the passageway. As he did, the marines in front of the elevator came to attention and saluted him.

He returned their salute. "You've done your ship proud today, gentlemen," he said. "You showed what marines are capable of. And you stayed true to yourselves. Good work."

"Sir," Avery said, "Major Hancock was my friend. But he put these men in danger for his own greed. I couldn't stand for that, and neither could they."

"You did the right thing. But our work isn't done."

From Thatcher's little speech over the *Charger*'s loudspeakers, Hancock had likely concluded his captain would come at him from the corridor behind. That was what Thatcher had wanted him to think, but it was only partly true.

He would also come from the bridge itself—something he was sure the former marine commander wouldn't expect, since it required lifting the solid-core barriers protecting the citadel, which would expose Candle and his bridge officers for the time it would take marines to charge through the bridge.

But Thatcher ordered Candle to have his officers take what cover they could on the far side of the area, with their sidearms drawn. "Don't shoot unless you have to," he told them.

Whether Hancock expected the move or not, opening up the citadel worked. Emmons rushed into the bridge with three squads of marines, and Avery flanked Hancock from the corridor with another three squads.

None of the marines or pirates with Hancock attempted to surrender, instead fighting to the last and forcing their attackers to kill them. Maybe Hancock had kept the real mutineers with him, and maybe those marines had acknowledged to themselves what they really were—traitors. If that was so, then in a sense their refusal to surrender was the most honorable thing they could have done. A man like that didn't truly deserve the opportunity to redeem himself, even though Thatcher would have offered that opportunity.

But none of those marines pretended to a cause any greater than their own greed. And they died like swine in the bloodbath that followed, which claimed every one of them, and no one else.

CHAPTER TWENTY-SEVEN

Aboard the *New Jersey*
Sable System, Dupliss Region
Earth Year 2290

THATCHER DID MOLL THE COURTESY OF SALUTING HIM AS HE disembarked his shuttle into the *Jersey*'s tiny starboard docking bay, which was just big enough to hold Attack Shuttle Two and a single visiting craft.

"Commander." Moll returned the salute, the halogens making his bare head gleam. "At ease."

Thatcher folded his hands behind his back, relaxing his stance. Since Sunder structured its corporate hierarchy along a proper military rank system, Thatcher was more than happy to respect Moll's rank by saluting first. Too many Cluster PMCs didn't use ranks at all.

But Moll *did* work for a different corp altogether—within a separate chain of command—and that corp was assisting Frontier. It wouldn't be wise to place the coming operation under Moll's authority. Which left them in a somewhat delicate situation.

Their eyes remained locked on each other's well after the salute, each man waiting for the other to break contact.

Moll sniffed sharply. "During the recent engagement, I was given to wondering why a Sunder destroyer, captained by a CEO, was expected to follow orders from a Frontier commander in charge of a light cruiser. Especially considering some of the reckless tactics you employed. I did not want to endanger our cause, so I played along, but I must admit it gave me pause."

"Perhaps that's something we can address at today's meeting. Won't you come with me?" Thatcher extended his arm toward the hatch.

"By all means. After you." The large man raised his own hand to indicate the portal.

Clearing his throat, Thatcher wrenched his gaze away and stalked to the hatch, which he pulled open by the handle. "After *you*," he said, holding open the hatch as he eyed Moll once more. The CEO returned Thatcher's gaze with a sardonic grin and strode through, ducking slightly. This time, he was the first to break eye contact.

Thatcher nodded to himself and followed Moll through. "Ms. Rose awaits us in the *Jersey*'s conference room, as does Commander Pat Frailey."

"I surmised as much. Considering I'm here to meet with them."

It didn't escape Thatcher how Moll tried to minimize him by implying he wasn't here to meet with him. But since they walked alone, the remark could only diminish him if he allowed it to. *He's trying to knock me off-balance before the meeting begins.*

"I've met captains like you before." Moll didn't turn to make the remark, instead keeping his eyes on the corridor ahead. "I've watched their careers catch fire for a time, only to sputter out in the cold void of the Cluster."

"What sort of captain do you mean?"

"The sort who thinks tactics will keep him safe. Usually, this kind of captain was patted on the head by his instructors all through his training and told what a smart boy he is. Clever tactics may fly in Earth Local Space, where the mommy state is never too far, ready with its super-ships to swoop in and save the day. But things are different here on the Cluster's outskirts, and tactics will only get you so far. If they're all you're playing with, then sooner or later you'll face an implacable foe who has you right where he wants you. And he will end you."

"Have you ever had the opportunity to warn such a captain about this pattern you've identified?" Thatcher kept his eyes straight ahead as well.

"Not before today."

"Then please let me say what an honor it is to give you the chance. And also what a privilege it will be to watch the reflection in your eyes as *my* career grows into an inferno that consumes the entire Dawn Cluster."

Moll did look at him now, his beard twitching as he gave a slight smile and nodded. "We shall see."

When they entered the conference room, Veronica Rose and Commander Frailey were already deep in discussion about what Frontier's next move should be.

"I don't think we can afford the time it would take to effect any further repairs," Rose was saying. "Hello, Commander Thatcher. And Captain Moll. Thank you for joining us."

"By all means." The Sunder CEO jerked a chair back and straddled it, openly appraising Commander Frailey as he did. Frailey reddened, lowering her gaze to the conference table.

His conduct appears much less formal than our first meeting, Thatcher reflected as he took a seat at the head of the table, opposite Rose.

The Frontier CEO shot Moll a sidelong glance, which he showed no sign of noticing. "We were just discussing whether to linger in Sable while we fully repair our ships." At Rose's words, Moll's eyes finally left Frailey's face for hers.

"Didn't we settle that already?" Thatcher was trying not to glare at Moll as he spoke. "The *Charger* will require a dry dock, but she's still operational. So are the other ships that have gathered. We need to strike without delay, before Reardon can further cement its footing." In addition to Frailey's *Boxer*, nine more Frontier ships had arrived in the Sable System since they'd left Frailey here—five corvettes, three frigates, and another light cruiser.

Rose shook her head. "There's been a development, Commander. Your XO's just informed me that another Frontier vessel has arrived in Sable: the *Lancer*, another cruiser. She's the latest to try poking her head into the Freedom System, and she met with the most violent response yet. It seems Reardon's less reluctant to reveal its collusion with pirates than we assumed. A mix of Reardon and pirate ships chased the *Lancer* out of the system, inflicting considerable damage. Other than the *Jersey* and the *Victorious*, she's now the most powerful ship we have at our disposal, which puts the question of repairs back on the table."

"What damage did she take?"

"All her port-side laser batteries are gone except one, her aft autoturrets were destroyed, and she's been reduced to sixty-four percent thrust capacity. Not to mention having her cargo bay blown out, along with everything inside it that wasn't bolted down. Without a repair and resupply, she'll be a burden on the rest of our force."

Thatcher stared at the bulkhead beyond Rose's shoulder for a moment as he considered the information. "I say we leave for Freedom regardless. The *Lancer* can form part of our reserve."

"There's more, Commander. With the pirates they've brought into Freedom, Reardon now outnumbers us two-to-one."

"Yes, and in the time it takes to repair and restock a cruiser, they'll add five more ships to their force. If not ten. The *Lancer* has taken some damage—so be it. She will belong to our reserve force."

"Can someone tell me why he keeps talking about a reserve force?" The way Moll emphasized the last two words seemed to imply the idea of such a force was as ridiculous as a swimming pool on a warship. "We don't have the luxury of a reserve. We have sixteen ships to their thirty-two, if your *Lancer*'s report is to be believed. Hitting hard and fast is our only chance."

Rose looked back and forth between Thatcher and Moll, apparently at a loss for words. Frailey showed no interest in intervening, even though she held the same rank as Thatcher.

But Thatcher had plenty to say. "I'm glad you offered your input, Captain Moll." He extended his hand toward the Sunder CEO, tapping the table for emphasis. "It reminds me that I need to make something clear, before we deploy to Freedom. You are merely a unit in this force, and you will do exactly as you're told, without question. This is a Frontier operation, and while we greatly appreciate Sunder's aid, I'm sure you understand we can't give another corp authority over how the coming engagement will go. Not when it's so crucial to our company's future."

"I'm putting my ship on the line," Moll shot back, his face stony. "As well as my crew, and even my corp, considering I'm its *CEO*. I'm entitled to *some* say over how we proceed."

"Your input will be given its due consideration. But we'll have the final say on tactical matters." Thatcher placed a slight emphasis on the word "tactical," as a callback to their conversation in the corridor. "We also reserve the right to withhold what our tactics will be until the moment we execute them."

Moll shook his head, sneering as he turned to Rose. "Why is this *employee* speaking for Frontier Security?"

Several seconds passed as Rose stared down the long table at

Thatcher. He'd crossed a line again, he knew. She couldn't be happy with him taking the reins for Frontier's relationship with Sunder, even for a minute. But if they were to maintain combat effectiveness, someone had to put Moll in his place, and Rose was too diplomatic to do it.

"I tend to agree with the commander, Captain."

Thatcher's eyebrows shot up, his shock the rough equal of Moll's scandalized expression.

"My father often stressed the importance of having unity of command." Rose folded her hands on the tabletop. "If we designate two battle commanders, with two completely different ideas of how an engagement should go, then we will only confuse our crews. And this *is* a Frontier matter. I'm sure you would say similar things, Captain, were our roles reversed."

"Fine." Moll's clenched fists sat in stark contrast with his level tone. "But surely you don't mean to make *him* the commander of your force. He's barely two months into his first command."

"True. Yet, Commander Thatcher's come through three engagements now without suffering any losses, despite consistent long odds. He came highly recommended by a U.S. Fleet admiral. I'm inclined to trust him."

After the meeting, Rose saw Moll to the starboard docking bay, leaving Thatcher to walk Frailey to the port bay. *Probably a smart move.* Leaving Thatcher alone with Moll again likely wouldn't do much for intercorporate relations.

"Thank you kindly for your hospitality, Commander." Frailey saluted.

He returned it. "It was a pleasure to have you aboard. Hopefully we have the opportunity again soon, at a less tumultuous time."

"I hope so. Although, I'm beginning to doubt there are many of those left."

With their visitors departed, Rose sent him a message requesting his presence in her cargo bay office.

"You said what needed to be said," she said when he appeared at her desk. "But you need to stop putting your mark on our relationships with outside parties."

Thatcher said nothing. He appreciated what she was saying, but he refused to apologize for what had to be done.

The Frontier CEO released a sigh. "No offense, Commander, but I'm beginning to think running this company will be a lot easier when I have an office again that isn't located in your cargo hold."

"That…may well be, Ms. Rose," he admitted, and cleared his throat. "I'm sure it's occurred to you already, but I believe Moll wants more from this operation than merely securing the Cluster's northwest. It also gives him the chance to wipe an old rival from the board. Reardon's been a thorn in Sunder's side for decades. Or so Mr. Mittelman tells me."

"Mittelman's right. Sunder's using us as surely as we're using them."

"Well, at least we're being honest about it." Thatcher paused, considering his next words carefully. "I noticed you didn't bring up the possibility that the Xanthic could show up in Freedom System to help Reardon. If they helped the pirates in battle, why not Pegg?"

Rose nodded slowly. "I considered mentioning it. But I still don't trust Moll, and I'd prefer Frailey not know, either. The fewer people that know about the aliens' presence in the Cluster, the less chance of it getting out and causing widespread panic."

"What if they do come?"

"Then we'll have to deal with it. You'll be in command of this mission, Commander, and you're briefed on the matter. That will have to be enough." Rose shrugged. "Maybe the Xanthic have decided to stick to the shadows, for now. That's what they've done so far."

Thatcher nodded. "I hope you're right. Could you ask Mittelman to come to my office? He doesn't appear to be answering my messages."

Rose gave a somewhat wry smile. "Sounds like him. I'll instruct him to come and speak with you, Commander."

CHAPTER TWENTY-EIGHT

Aboard the *New Jersey*
Vinea System, Dupliss Region
Earth Year 2290

THE WEEKLY CAPTAIN'S INSPECTION FELL ON THE DAY BEFORE they were due to enter Freedom System, and Thatcher had a strong suspicion that much of the crew had hoped he would skip it, with an engagement looming large.

Whether they actually believed *I'd skip it....*

Well, maybe they had believed it. But if so, they didn't yet know their captain very well.

As for his division officers, they seemed to have better sense than that.

"Group, atten-tion!" called Lieutenant Dolores Anthony, the *Jersey*'s senior supply officer. The entire supply division snapped to attention.

"Hand sal-ute," Anthony boomed. Every supply crewmember saluted their captain, and he returned it.

"Order arms."

They returned their arms to their sides.

With that, Thatcher marched up and down their ranks, making sure their boots shone and that their uniforms were lint-free and creased where they should be.

Most civilians didn't understand the military's obsession with immaculate presentation. In fact, Thatcher was convinced that many in the military didn't, either. If it hadn't been for his grandfather, he might never have properly understood it.

"Hospital corners," Edward Thatcher had said in his soft-spoken way. "Polished buttons. Boots that shine. It all seems silly, to the casual observer. But combat effectiveness starts with those boots, Tad. When a soldier grows sloppy, his unit will soon follow. Disorder has a way of sneaking in from the corners of life, if you let it. Soon after, it'll spread to everything, sewing the seeds of your defeat."

After Thatcher finished inspecting the ranks, he moved on to the lockers, offices, and other spaces the supply crew were responsible for. Each door he approached had a man or woman of the division standing by to open it for him.

A voice came on over the ship's 1MC, and he halted, staring up at a nearby loudspeaker in consternation.

"People of the Dawn Cluster, I bring you a message of hope —a promise, but also a warning. I am Veronica Rose, CEO of Frontier Security, and today my corp stands at a crossroads. Everyone listening to these words has arrived at that same fork in the road, whether you realize it or not."

Ah. He'd forgotten that Rose had asked his permission to broadcast her message throughout the ship at the same time she transmitted it to every other instant comm unit in the Cluster. Likewise, he'd forgotten to tell her not to do it during his inspection.

Oh, well. There was no reason not to continue.Maybe Rose's words would even lend the process extra gravity.

As he left one office for the next, the CEO continued her first Cluster-wide broadcast. The first of many, if the constant talk from her and Moll about the importance of messaging was any indication.

"The wormhole to Earth has slammed shut, and this bountiful cluster has become our prison. We are cut off from the planet that birthed us, just as our home's greatest hour of need has arrived. How can we conduct business of any kind, knowing humanity needs us? How can we move forward even as Earth Local Space falls under attack by the insectile Xanthic?"

Thatcher's gaze roved around the office for signs of disorganization—a coffee stain, a dusty shelf. Any indication its occupant had started to relax the never-ending vigilance required to maintain order.

"At first, it seems impossible. Wouldn't any decent person fall to despair, knowing their brothers and sisters were alone against a merciless foe? Shouldn't we simply give up?" Rose paused, her intake of breath audible over the loudspeaker. "But I tell you now we must never give up. To do that would amount to a betrayal—not just of Earth, but of all the people scattered throughout the Dawn Cluster, colonist and spacer alike.

"Our duty to protect and further human prosperity does not end with the closing of the wormhole. It only grows more urgent. Because there are those who would use the wormhole's closing as cover to exploit the innocent—to gain wealth and power off the backs of those who cannot defend themselves. And they grow bolder with every day the wormhole remains closed. Reardon Interstellar is such a villain. In their insane lust for profit at the expense of all else, they have endangered colonists throughout Dupliss Region by aligning themselves with pirates. These criminals have flooded into the region at Reardon's invitation. Mere days ago, we prevented a gang from taking control of Prosperity Station, a civilian Helio base."

Everything was in order, with nothing out of place. Thatcher gave the office's occupant an approving nod and departed for the next. He wondered idly what the office had looked like before he'd taken command of the *Jersey*.

"Frontier does not intend to take these gross transgressions lying down. We have partnered with Simon Moll of Sunder Incorporated, and together we intend to redress every injustice without mercy. Despite being an American corp, Reardon Interstellar and its rogue CEO Ramon Pegg do not believe in truth, justice, and freedom. That is no matter. Because we are prepared to enforce those values throughout Dupliss—at the business end of a laser battery, if necessary. In doing so, we will grind Reardon to dust."

Silence reigned throughout the ship. Thatcher had drawn to a stop between offices to hear Rose's final, fiery words, and now his gaze fell on Lieutenant Anthony. Unbidden, a smile spread across his face.

Bold. Passionate. And more than a little over-the-top. He glanced back at the nearest loudspeaker. *It was probably just what we needed.*

CHAPTER TWENTY-NINE

Aboard the *New Jersey*
Vinea System, Dupliss Region
Earth Year 2290

"THAT WAS QUITE A SPEECH YOU GAVE THIS MORNING." Thatcher walked beside the Frontier CEO with his hands folded behind his back. He'd wanted to take his ship's—and his crew's —temperature one last time before he took the *New Jersey* into battle. "I didn't know you had it in you."

Veronica Rose gave him a wan smile. "If I went around talking like that all the time, I doubt many people would want to be around me. But it seems to have done the trick for getting the Dawn Cluster riled up."

"You've gotten responses back already?"

"Indeed I have. We may be outnumbered when we enter Freedom, but with the number of corps who sent us messages of support, our ranks dwarf Reardon's."

"If only we could fire messages of support at the enemy."

They reached a dead end—one of the *Jersey*'s special quiet places, the kind of spot where he liked to periodically bring a random member of the crew, to ask about his impression of the ship, and his appreciation for his own role within her. Instead of turning around to continue their tour of the light cruiser, Thatcher and Rose stopped, facing each other.

"You should know that even some Chinese corporations have signaled their support, despite our talk of truth and freedom. So don't underestimate the power of words in this new environment, Commander. Stranded here in the Cluster, cut off from the UNC's main fleet...the instant comm unit may well become the highest source of authority in play."

"Have your people managed to reverse engineer the device yet?" He knew she'd brought a couple of her techs over from the *Squall* for that purpose.

"Not yet. They want to dismantle it, take a look at the guts, but I'm hesitant to let them do that until we have a little more stability. Until then, the unit remains a black box, leaving us guessing at how it's able to transmit messages faster than light."

He nodded, tamping down an urge to lean against the bulk-head. It still seemed unusual to allow himself too much repose around his new boss.

To his surprise, she *did* lean a shoulder against the spotless metal surface, one hand resting comfortably on her hip while she ran the other through her whip-straight midnight hair. "I haven't been invited to dine with you since boarding the *Jersey*, Commander. I know things have been hectic, but perhaps after the battle. It's likely we would benefit from a more casual setting, and the ability to speak a little more freely."

Thatcher's cheek spasmed, and he fought to school his face to blankness. The CEO's words made sense—they likely *would* be able to make more headway on Frontier's direction in a more relaxed setting; one that didn't include potential spies. But it had been Rose's body language while making the suggestion that set him on edge.

"I...should go."

Rose's eyebrows lifted. She wasn't one to overreact, but he could tell she was surprised.

"Last-minute preparations," he muttered, tearing his gaze away from her sapphire eyes and stalking down the passageway, leaving her alone in the private *cul-de-sac*.

Back in his cabin, drawing ragged breaths, he picked up his framed photo of Lin from beside his rack. She hadn't wanted to have a photo taken while pregnant, but he'd made getting one a priority before he left for the Dawn Cluster.

He'd wanted a new photo badly. One that showed her *and* their unborn son. In it, she had both hands over her swollen stomach, and her smile beamed radiantly into the camera, lighting up her otherwise serene face.

"I'm coming back to you," he told the photo. "And I'll grind the Xanthic to dust to keep you safe."

CHAPTER THIRTY

Aboard the *Victorious*
Carillon System, Dupliss Region
Earth Year 2290

"Ten minutes from the jump gate into Freedom, sir." The operations officer cleared her throat, signaling her agitation.

But she was only mirroring her captain's emotions, as Moll's CIC crew so often did. That happened when you had complete respect from your subordinates. Not to mention complete control over them. *Something Thatcher's a long way from having.*

"Acknowledged." He drummed his fingers on his chair's armrest, in the protracted way he knew set his officers on edge. That was good. Nervous officers were watchful officers, and though he rarely unleashed his ire, they'd experienced it enough to know they didn't like it.

"I don't believe he intends to send the order to stagger our forces, Theo."

His XO nodded, mouth a thin line. "It seems you're right, Captain."

Standard jump zone evasion entailed sending in an eWar ship

first as a scout, to jam any waiting ships and then rush to the corresponding jump gate to report back to the origin system. Moll frowned. "So we're meant to send everything into a potential slaughter, with a very good chance Pegg has his ships positioned around the jump zone on the other side, just waiting to turn it into a shooting gallery. Thatcher hasn't even given orders to implement countermeasures to account for the possibility."

Theodore Lane made a sympathetic sound.

Moll cursed under his breath. He'd told Thatcher to his face that he wasn't ready for the Cluster. Still, he'd had no idea it was this bad.

A career that blazed into an inferno, wasn't it? Hell, I'm not sure he'll even manage to light the match.

"I guess it's up to me to make sure this operation isn't a total disaster." Moll turned to his left. "Ops, get me the *New Jersey.*"

"Aye, sir."

Seconds later, Thatcher appeared in the state-of-the-art holotank at the front of the CIC. "Captain Moll," he said with a calmness that bordered on arrogance.

"Commander. You do realize Reardon has almost certainly laid an ambush for us on the other side of that jump gate?"

"I considered the possibility. But I don't think it's likely."

Moll exchanged looks with his XO, not bothering to conceal his incredulity. "Why *wouldn't* Pegg concentrate his forces on the jump zone? Wouldn't you?"

"Probably, but I'm an honest actor, and Pegg isn't. As you know, his company is in a tenuous position. Certainly, they've gained new pirate allies, but I doubt trust flows freely between the two parties. Certainly, Pegg wouldn't trust them to hold Oasis by themselves. There's also the fact that there were two jump gates we might have used to enter Freedom. Pegg doesn't know which route we chose, since we haven't left any pirate ships operational to report that intel to him, and I very much doubt the pirates have access to instant communications yet. Pegg won't want to split his fleet to cover both gates."

"Still not convinced." Moll's chin rested on his hand. "Even with his forces split in half, an ambush at the jump zones would still prove effective with our ships trickling in."

Thatcher tilted his head, his expression still irritatingly serene. "I don't think you're properly factoring the planet into your analysis. Oasis represents Pegg's most important bargaining chip, against us and against the UNC, in the unlikely event they come knocking. He won't give up that leverage lightly—won't abandon it to cover two gates, with the risk of treacherous pirates or even a third adversary claiming and securing the planet against him while he does. No, he'll have his ships huddled around Oasis like frightened sheep. And that's where we'll take them."

"So you're a mind reader. You know exactly what Pegg will do—better than he does, even!" Moll chuckled and shook his head. "Very well, Commander. It's your funeral. Just know that the *Victorious* will not be the first to go through that gate. If you insist on taking such a foolhardy risk, then we'll bring up the rear."

"By all means. This *is* a Frontier operation, after all. The *Squall* will transition first, with the *New Jersey* close on her stern. Our eWar ship has orders to execute an omnidirectional jamming burst in the unlikely event Pegg has laid a jump zone ambush. In that event, all ships must scatter and regroup else-where inside the Freedom System. But I'm sure I don't need to relay basic jump zone evasion to you, Captain."

Moll felt his torso stiffen. *So he is taking precautions.* Whether he knew it or not, Thatcher had just made a fool of Moll in front of his officers.

"Very well," he choked out. "Let's proceed, then, Commander."

"I intend to. Thatcher out." The blasted man vanished from the holotank.

An uneasy silence settled over the CIC. Moll could understand why. His crew wasn't used to seeing their captain in want of the upper hand.

He glanced at his XO. "Thatcher won't last the year, unfortunately. He has no idea how ruthless things get on this side of the galaxy. The Dawn Cluster will chew him up and spit him out."

"Yes, sir," was all his XO said.

Moll gritted his teeth and waited for the first ships to transition through the jump gate.

CHAPTER THIRTY-ONE

Aboard the *New Jersey*
Freedom System, Dupliss Region
Earth Year 2290

THE JUMP GATE GAVE THE *JERSEY* A COSMIC SHOVE, SENDING IT hurtling between two distant stars. Less than a minute later, the universe resolved from the gray storm cloud of transition to the star-speckled expanse that had been Thatcher's domain since he graduated from the academy thirteen years ago.

"You were right, sir," Lucy Guerrero said, with a note of satisfaction in her otherwise tremulous voice. "There are no ships covering the jump zone."

Thatcher nodded. He got the sense Guerrero was about as fond of Simon Moll as he was. He also knew she felt even more anxious than usual, with the knowledge her husband and children were just half a system away.

"Give me the situation around Oasis as soon as you have it, Guerrero. In the meantime, order the *Squall* to begin assembling the outrider outside the jump zone."

"Aye, sir."

SCOTT BARTLETT

As he'd told Moll, Thatcher sent the eWar ship through the jump gate first as a precaution against ambush. But hard on the *New Jersey*'s heels came a frigate, a corvette, and a logistics ship —all Frontier vessels that had joined Commander Frailey in Sable while Thatcher and Moll had fought pirates in Epact. These would form the outrider, a small force intended to harass the main enemy and sew confusion, with the aim of overloading Ramon Pegg's attention as his ships reached out to him for help, intel, and new orders.

Thatcher had selected the outrider ships mostly for their speed. They all displaced far less mass than a ship like the *Jersey* or the *Victorious*, since as well as being smaller, all four boasted cutting-edge nanofiber structures. They also had the necessary inertial compensator upgrades to protect their crews at the higher velocities.

As protocol demanded, his Nav and Helm officers collaborated to bring the *Jersey* outside the jump zone, despite how vanishingly unlikely it was that one of the arriving ships would jump on top of them. It took the better part of twenty minutes for every vessel to transition, and as promised, both Sunder ships brought up the rear.

A more spiteful man would have found an excuse to speak to Moll, to rub the absence of an ambush in his face. *Rose would murder me if I did that.*

He hadn't been idle as the warships trickled through, however, instead sending orders for each to assemble according to the role he'd assigned them: outrider, reserve, or main attack. In fact, his outrider was already underway toward Oasis.

Bryce Sullivan looked up from the Nav station. "Our course toward Oasis is ready for the Helm and for distribution to the other captains, sir."

"Very well, lieutenant. Send it to Helm and to Ops to be forwarded. Stand by to alter the course as new intel comes in."

"Aye, sir."

Thatcher had chosen to arrange his forces as he had based on a theory about how the Reardon ships would behave. But as his cruiser accelerated toward the planet, which he knew to be surrounded by at least twice his fleet's number, the hairs on the back of his neck stirred in anticipation. *I was right about the ambush. But what if Pegg's already anticipated* my *psychology, and has set a trap to exploit it?*

Like Moll, Pegg had been fighting pirates—and other corps, if the rumors were true—in the Dawn Cluster for decades. That placed them among humanity's most experienced space warriors, while Thatcher had barely just arrived.

Moll's words rang in his ears: *I've met captains like you before. I've watched their careers catch fire for a time, only to sputter out in the cold void of the Cluster.*

But Thatcher was in charge of this operation, not Moll. That was how it had to be. And so, he could only trust his gut, which was telling him that space warfare was still a stunted thing, no matter how much experience Pegg and Moll had. The Sunder CEO had admitted to a disdain for "clever tactics," and that outlook made sense for corps that had always enjoyed superior firepower over their pirate adversaries. But now that corps had begun to openly fight other corps, something more would be needed.

Guerrero's hands picked up speed as they flew across her console. "Sensor data is coming in from Oasis, sir. Sending it to your console now."

"Acknowledged." Thatcher watched as his holoscreen populated with the locations of Reardon ships.

A sigh of relief escaped him. As he'd predicted, Reardon's behavior continued to reflect how vital holding Oasis had become to them. Pegg had divided twenty-four of his ships between the six Helio bases distantly orbiting the planet, with the remaining twelve in close planetary orbit.

Clearly, he expected Thatcher to head directly toward the

planet, for fear that Pegg would harm the colonists. If Thatcher did that, then Pegg would tighten the noose, calling his ships from the Helio bases to outflank and destroy the Frontier-Sunder forces.

Thatcher *did* intend to make directly for the planet—or rather, his outrider would do that. And while the *Squall* and her companions kept the enemy fleet commander's hands full, Thatcher would fall upon the ships at the nearest Helio base.

"Guerrero, get me fleetwide. I would give the next order myself."

"Fleetwide channel is open, sir."

Thatcher inclined his head. "All ships consigned to the main attack force will make for the Helio base whose designation I will send. The outrider will maintain course toward Oasis, to jam Reardon's main force and otherwise keep them busy, pulling back if they give chase and harassing them again once they disengage. All captains should stay ready to receive and implement new orders promptly as the engagement progresses. Thatcher out."

Almost immediately, Guerrero turned toward him wearing a blank expression. "The *Victorious* is hailing us, sir."

Thatcher's jaw clenched. He should have predicted that Moll would question him at every turn. Briefly, he considered having their conversation in his office, but he couldn't bring himself to leave the CIC. Not at a time like this.

"Everyone, remain focused on your tasks. Put him through, Guerrero."

The Sunder CEO appeared once more in the CIC's holotank, his eyes ablaze. "You've gone from reckless to irresponsible, Commander."

"That's an interesting opinion. But I'll have to reiterate to you: this is a Frontier operation, and we intend to conduct it as we see fit."

"Pegg has Oasis at his mercy. Those colonists' survival depends on his whims, right now."

Thatcher gave a dry chuckle. "I doubt Ramon Pegg is as whimsical as you seem to think. If he harms those colonists, every major power in the Cluster will be gunning for him. His corp would perish within a month."

"It'll perish anyway if he loses this battle. You don't think he'll play his last card, if he's forced to?"

"I do not, since it *wouldn't* be his last card. There's also the possibility of surrendering and negotiating."

"He won't do that."

"I think he will. And since I happen to be in charge of this operation, we will proceed under that assumption."

"You should at least send the reserve force to accompany the outrider toward the planet."

"That would defeat the purpose of a reserve. You have your orders, Captain Moll. Thatcher out." He nodded at Guerrero.

Moll's reddening face disappeared from the holotank, and for a moment Thatcher contemplated the tactical display that replaced him.

The Sunder captain's apparent concern for the civilians would play well with anyone who heard of it, and Thatcher's focus on tactics could easily be spun as cold and unfeeling.

But he remembered Moll's enthusiasm for messaging and rhetoric. While his outward conduct seemed admirable, his conviction that Reardon would be willing to sacrifice the colonists told Thatcher something else.

It told him that if Moll was in Pegg's position, he *would* be willing to kill the colonists. It was just as Hans Mittelman had said during their final meeting before they entered Freedom System:

Moll was obsessed with winning. At any cost.

CHAPTER THIRTY-TWO

Aboard the *New Jersey*
Freedom System, Dupliss Region
Earth Year 2290

"OPS, SIGNAL OUR ATTACK FORCE TO SPLIT INTO ITS predesignated squadrons. The *Jersey*'s squadron will pass to the Helio base's right, with the *Victorious*' squadron passing on the left. All ships will follow a course perpendicular to the Helio base's turrets, with engines at sixty percent power. We target the frigate first."

"Aye, sir."

Thatcher dragged two fingers across his holoscreen, viewing the station they hurtled toward from various angles. If it hadn't been for the Helio base's turrets, the four ships stationed there would pose minimal danger to his eight-strong attack force. Only the Reardon frigate was a true warship—two of the others were converted freighters, and the last was a former mining vessel.

But the bases posed a problem. Pegg had enjoyed plenty of time to send his marines into them, commandeering them to cement his control of Oasis.

We have to strike fast. The Squall *can only keep the main Reardon force occupied for so long.*

"Tactical, target the frigate with our primary, and be ready to follow up with autoturrets and even Hellborns if needed. We must destroy her in one pass. Guerrero, relay that order to the others."

"Aye, sir," said both Ortega and Guerrero.

The frigate already had her shields up, but when lasers lanced out from six warships, the force field rippled madly. Turrets sprayed solid-core rounds at the attacking vessels, but their transverse velocity kept them safe from most of the projectiles. As for *Lightfoot* and *Paragon*—the latter being the other Frontier eWar vessel that had rendezvoused in Sable—they kept well out of firing range, passing the station at a greater distance than the others in case their support was needed.

The enemy shield went down, and six primary lasers slammed into her hull. She lasted only a few seconds under the heavy assault, and then she ruptured, blowing apart in a way that would make her wreck difficult to salvage.

Thatcher tapped furiously at his console. "Guerrero, all ships will switch to the target I'm designating."

"Aye, sir."

His main attack force drew level with the station, and soon their firing solutions would become unworkable until they swung back around. But six beams lanced out again, and the targeted freighter burst apart immediately.

That was overkill. He should have designated two separate targets. But his battle group was pulling past the Helio base, and he could do nothing about his blunder now. "Ortega, order all port-side gunner crews to target the base's turrets. Tell Major Avery to stand by to launch Attack Shuttle One and board the station." After Avery's performance aboard the *Charger*, Thatcher had gotten Rose's permission to promote him to Major and take over command of the *Jersey's* marine company.

Before Ortega could acknowledge the order, Thatcher turned once more toward Guerrero. "Order all ships to decelerate in preparation to execute an artificial orbital maneuver. Both squadrons will pass each other and come around the opposite side of the station."

Both his tactical and operations officer bent to their work. Artificial orbits were largely handled by a ship's AI. The station was far too small for his ships to orbit it in fact, but through a series of thrusters firing in sequence, such an orbit could be simulated, for the purpose of maintaining transverse velocity relative to the blazing turret batteries.

But the *Jersey*'s gunner crews were already cutting down on those batteries' numbers, and gunners from the other ships had joined them. As Thatcher's squadrons sailed past each other to come around once more, he surveyed the battlespace with satisfaction. Yes, the station had lent the four enemy ships sharper teeth, but it also hurt them in a way that proved more important: it kept them anchored to a single point, making it easy for Thatcher to outmaneuver them as he picked apart their formation.

"Target the nearest enemy vessel with a Hellborn, Ortega. Guerrero, have the *Victorious* fire two at the same target."

The salvo saw to the converted freighter nicely, blowing it into multiple twisted sections.

"The remaining enemy ship is hailing us, sir," his operations officer said. "They wish to surrender."

"Very well. All ships will hold their fire. Tell the surrendering vessel they have five minutes to don pressure suits and evacuate their ship through her airlock, to be picked up later. Ortega, order the gunners to disable her thrusters and weapons."

No one spoke up to question the wisdom of waiting while the freighter crew evacuated, but Thatcher could tell by the way several of his CIC crew shifted their weight that they weren't completely comfortable with the idea. So far the *Squall* and the rest of the outrider had kept Pegg busy, but that wouldn't last forever. Besides, the people he'd spared were almost certainly pirates.

Nevertheless, Thatcher didn't consider the five minutes wasted, and it wasn't only because he didn't consider it very American to shoot enemies after they'd surrendered. If Frontier earned a reputation for doing that, they would soon reach a point where their enemies refused to ever surrender to them, knowing Frontier would only kill them if they did.

That meant every adversary would fight them to the last, and victory would mean inflicting total slaughter, whereas allowing enemies to surrender could achieve it much sooner, with far less loss on both sides.

Over the longterm, treating prisoners of war respectfully amounted to a force multiplier that Thatcher refused to give up.

Guerrero turned. "Major Avery is ready, sir. Shall I tell him he's clear to launch?"

"Affirmative."

Seconds later, the entire ship trembled with Attack Shuttle One's departure.

CHAPTER THIRTY-THREE

Aboard the *New Jersey*
Freedom System, Dupliss Region
Earth Year 2290

AT THATCHER'S ORDER, SULLIVAN HAD A COURSE READY FOR the moment the converted freighter's crew had finished evacuating.

"Bring engines to full formation speed, Helm. I want to reach the next base quickly, so we'll need to decelerate hard on the other end. Ops, tell the others to do the same."

"Aye, sir." Guerrero glanced at him. "Captain, the ships stationed at Helio bases are moving. All except the vessels positioned around the base we're targeting."

"Acknowledged," Thatcher said, scrutinizing the tactical display as a bead of sweat ran down his forehead. He refused to wipe it away, not wanting to spread his uneasiness to his crew.

Apparently Pegg had managed to keep a better grasp on the battlespace than Thatcher had anticipated. Only he could have given an order like this. Three Reardon strike groups were abandoning their Helio bases to head for the planet, where Thatcher's outrider was having an outsized effect, while a fourth group moved to back up the ships at the Helio base approached by the main Frontier attack force.

"The four enemy ships already positioned around our target station are spreading out, sir," Guerrero said. "It seems they want to prevent us from establishing a favorable transverse velocity."

Thatcher nodded. They wouldn't be able to thwart this base's turrets as they had the last. He could almost hear Moll laughing inside his destroyer as his sensors registered the same thing.

Clever tactics will only get you so far…

That was true—but only if you kept using the same tactics.

"Belay the order to decelerate. Nav, I want you to devise a new course to send to the Helm as well as our other ships. At the moment before it becomes impossible to remain outside the firing range of the ships gathered around the target station, we will change course to do exactly that."

A brief silence, and Sullivan spoke: "What will be our new destination, sir?"

"The Helio base those ships just abandoned."

"Aye, sir."

The *New Jersey* sailed forward as the Reardon and pirate ships carried on with their maneuvers, angling to cast a wide net meant to intercept Thatcher's attack force. Pegg had reacted with admirable quickness, but it seemed the outrider's distraction had served a purpose: it had prevented the Reardon CEO from anticipating what Thatcher would do next.

Thatcher did not suffer from that shortcoming. He could see that Reardon was desperate to protect their remaining Helio bases, and that made sense. If Frontier took them, they could dig in, entrench their position, and wait for more company ships to arrive in-system—or even for other corps to come to their aid.

That didn't seem likely. Most Dawn Cluster corps were clearly against Reardon, but also embroiled in their own conflicts. Either way, Pegg couldn't afford to take the risk.

And so, when the main Frontier attack force changed course to scream past their original target, hurtling toward the freshly abandoned Helio base, the Reardon forces reacted by abandoning their formation and giving chase.

"Nav, calculate a deceleration profile that takes us just outside the firing range of our new target base."

"Aye, sir."

The enemy forces behaved exactly as he'd anticipated, stringing themselves across Thatcher's holoscreen tactical display in their desperate attempt to catch up to his forces, each ship's top speed taking it away from her fellows. *Just as the pirates did in Olent.* Clearly, some tactics had a longer shelf life than others. Not that the Reardon ships had much choice other than to pursue him with abandon, given how vital the Helio bases were to their control over Oasis.

"Prepare to reverse course and accelerate." Thatcher eyed the closest enemy craft, a modified patrol ship that probably benefited from upgraded thrusters or a nanofiber structure, judging by how it had outstripped its companions. *That won't serve you well, today.* "Fire a Hellborn the moment we reverse our trajectory, Ortega, and let's have the *Victorious* do the same."

"Aye, sir."

The *Jersey* came to a fleeting standstill before Sullivan brought her around to rocket back toward the oncoming ships. A Hellborn leapt from her single missile tube with the characteristic tremor.

Almost immediately, the target attempted evasive maneuvers, but with two computer-guided missiles incoming it was next to pointless. In the last few seconds its autoturrets flared up, trying to shoot the rockets down, but they failed. The first Hellborn blew apart the patrol ship's bow, and the second all but vaporized her.

"All ships are to close with the enemy at full formation speed, Guerrero." Unlike the Reardon and pirate vessels, *his* warships would hold formation by only sailing as quickly as their slowest craft's top speed.

"Aye, sir."

The enemy vessels attempted to modify their velocities and regroup, but with the Frontier formation bearing down on them, the damage was practically already done. Lasers flickered across the void like vengeful serpent tongues, and Hellborns leapt from their tubes to dash themselves on enemy hulls.

Only the last three Reardon ships managed to form up with each other, but against eight foes they stood little chance. What damage they managed to inflict before their destruction was quickly repaired with the help of the *Lightfoot*.

Now, I have a decision to make.

With eight more enemy ships wiped from the board, two Helio bases stood open to him, undefended except by their auto-turrets. He could take them, but he feared getting sandwiched between the turrets and Pegg's main force. In the last few minutes, the Reardon ships in planetary orbit had managed to take out the outrider's corvette, and now they were gunning for the frigate.

Thatcher didn't actually want to besiege Oasis by holding the Helio bases. Attempting that would be as risky to him as losing them would be to Pegg. Possibly more, if no corps came to Frontier's aid while pirates continued to flood in for Reardon.

Guerrero looked up from her console, and her next words pushed the dilemma from Thatcher's mind. "Sir, Reardon is hailing us. It's Ramon Pegg's destroyer—the *Eagle*."

CHAPTER THIRTY-FOUR

Aboard the *New Jersey*
Freedom System, Dupliss Region
Earth Year 2290

IF RAMON'S SHADED GLASSES WERE INTENDED TO HIDE HIS emotions, they weren't doing a very good job.

His hairless features contorted around the shades—eyebrows drawn down to hide their inner tips behind the lenses, shoulders bunched, and lips peeled back to reveal tightly clenched teeth.

"This is it," the Swede growled from the CIC holotank. "You've pushed us far enough. Surrender your ships or we'll lay waste to the colony."

At that, Guerrero jerked in her seat, going rigid as she clutched her chair's armrests. Luckily, Pegg couldn't see the lieutenant.

Thatcher forced himself to remain loose and relaxed. "You mean the same colony you are contracted to protect? You did kick Frontier out of the Oasis *Protectorate*, did you not? Are you aware of that word's meaning?"

"The Cluster's moved way past playing shepherd to a flock of colonist sheep, you dope. It's kill or be killed, now. We intend to kill. Unless you surrender your ships at once."

A puzzle piece clicked into place inside Thatcher's mind, and he suppressed the smile that threatened to spread across his face. "Tell me, Pegg. Are you aware the UNC is distributing instant comm units to corps throughout the Cluster?"

The Reardon CEO's scowl took on a note of confusion.

"I can see that you *aren't* aware. I suppose that shouldn't come as much of a surprise, considering you've managed to politically isolate yourself from almost the entire Cluster. Well, the UNC has indeed begun handing out the tech for instant communication across light years, and they gave one of its units to Frontier Security. That unit currently sits on the *New Jersey*, fully integrated with her existing systems. At any moment I choose, I can broadcast throughout the Cluster a recording of the remarks you just made about killing colonists."

"You're bluffing." Pegg's face whitened, in stark contradiction to his statement.

"No, Captain Pegg, I'm not. But we both know *you* are. The only thing worse than publicly contemplating the slaughter of innocents would be to actually do it. The Cluster's corps would band together and exterminate Reardon in a matter of months. You wanted us to surrender so that you could do away with us, and then portray what happened here however you wished. But now you know that isn't possible. So you can drop your charade about attacking colonists."

"It's no charade." Pegg leaned forward, cords standing out on his neck. "Last chance. Surrender now, or I'll do it. I'll kill them."

Lucy Guerrero twisted in her seat to stare at him with wide eyes. "Captain—"

"Be silent, Lieutenant." He understood how she felt, with her family vulnerable on the planet below. If Lin had been down there, he doubted he'd be keeping it together as well as this. But he knew he was right.

"Well?" Thatcher said after a long moment.

Pegg settled back into his chair. "You bastard."

"That's what I thought. Now that we have that nonsense out of the way, let's discuss more realistic options. I'm willing to make you an offer. Leave Dupliss."

That brought a sneer to Pegg's face. "Dupliss is mine, cretin."

"No, it isn't, and you're running on borrowed time. But there's a way for your corp to survive this intact. Take every Reardon ship and depart this region, never to return. Leave the pirates to us. Those are my terms, and they're the best you're going to get."

"You must be quite a poker player," Pegg said with a sardonic chuckle. "Here are *my* terms." With that, Pegg vanished from the holotank, and the transmission ended.

When Guerrero spoke, he thought he heard a measure of relief in her voice. "Sir, the Reardon ships in planetary orbit have just destroyed the outrider frigate and are now advancing on our position."

It seemed almost grotesque that his operations officer would feel relieved in the face of a second Frontier ship going down and an overwhelming enemy force moving on them. But at the same time, Thatcher could understand it. *Anything that takes her husband and children out of harm's way.*

It didn't matter. The true battle was about to begin. His true test. At twenty-four to fourteen, the enemy force still grossly outnumbered his. Yes, Thatcher had taken out twelve ships while losing only two from his outrider, but the vessels he'd destroyed had mostly been former private starships, stolen and converted by pirates. What remained were state-of-the-art warships, armed to the teeth and fielded by one of the Dawn Cluster's wealthiest corporations.

Pegg would throw Reardon Interstellar's full weight at him, now.

CHAPTER THIRTY-FIVE

Aboard the *New Jersey*
Freedom System, Dupliss Region
Earth Year 2290

"The enemy fleet is spreading out, sir. It appears they're attempting to outflank us."

"Acknowledged." Thatcher heard a certain flatness in his own voice—a distractedness he hoped didn't come across as worry to his crew.

But Reardon's maneuvers did concern him. Pegg was using Thatcher's own tactic against him by forcing him into a disadvantageous position. He would have liked to fall back to the one Helio base his marines had taken over, to use its remaining turrets to even the odds a little. But the Reardon flank on that side, *Jersey*'s starboard side, was moving to swiftly cut off that option. It was also too late to take one of the bases nearest him— Reardon would be atop them before they managed to get marines aboard.

Thatcher's outrider had lost its teeth with the destruction of its frigate and corvette, and the eWar and the logistics vessel had withdrawn to the planet's horizon, well out of Reardon's reach. "Have our reserve ships rally with the outrider at the Helio base we control, Guerrero. From there, they can flank the Reardon fleet, with the option of falling back to the station's turrets if needed."

"Aye, sir. Though it doesn't seem possible they can set up the flank before the engagement begins."

"I know." Thatcher studied his holoscreen's tactical display, breathing through the tension threatening to immobilize him. He'd arrived at one of those moments which his grandfather had always said separated good captains from great ones. The ability to stare down daunting odds, keep one's cool, and pull through— that was the stuff legends were made from.

Edward Thatcher's hoarse voice echoed through his head. "It will be hard, Tad. Harder than you can imagine. It will feel impossible. And there's a good chance you'll fail. Most do. But if there's ever a time to prove what you're really made of, that's it."

His grandfather had been right. Thatcher *hadn't* been able to imagine how hard it would be to keep his cool, because nothing he'd envisioned came close to this. But he was Tad Thatcher. The grandson of Edward Thatcher, hero of the first Xanthic Conflict. And he refused to let his story end in shameful defeat.

"Ops, order all ships to direct primary laserfire at the ship I'm designating." He selected a frigate on his holoscreen's 3D representation of the battlespace, and he sent it to Guerrero for distribution to the rest of his attack force.

A few seconds later, Guerrero turned to him, her frustration written across her brow. "The *Victorious* is hailing us again, sir."

Thatcher's stomach hardened, and it took him a moment to process what his Ops officer had said. *Now?* "Put it through."

When Moll appeared in the holotank, he appeared about as exasperated as Thatcher felt. "Can I ask what you think you're doing, telling us to target one of Reardon's lowest-value units?"

Thatcher's voice came out with an edge. "Captain Moll, you've been reminded multiple times that this is a Frontier operation that you are merely participating in—*not* commanding. You're endangering our forces by questioning my orders at such a critical time. And you're certainly *not* keeping up your end of the bargain."

"*You're* endangering us by failing to select high-value targets. We should focus on Pegg's destroyer first."

Thatcher shook his head, unable to believe he was having this argument. "No. Look at how Pegg keeps the *Eagle* toward the rear of the formation. He *hopes* we'll target it, so he can reverse thrust and draw us into a more vulnerable position. Even if we succeeded in neutralizing his destroyer, we would be relinquishing our best weapon—Pegg's awareness of his corp's vulnerable political position. Kill him, and the other Reardon crews would be left without direction. They'd behave like wild animals backed into a corner, and they'd attack with abandon. But with Pegg alive, we can pressure Reardon as a whole, and convince him to leave Freedom."

"Wait—*leave?* I thought we were here to destroy Reardon for good. You'd offer them the chance to leave?"

"*You* might have come to destroy Reardon. I came to save the colonists of Oasis, by any means necessary."

Moll's nostrils flared. "This is a blatant violation of our—"

Veronica's Rose voice cut into the conversation. "Captain Moll, right now *you* are violating our deal. Thatcher's right. You're supposed to follow his orders, not stand in the way of victory."

Moll cocked his head upward, even though neither of them could see Rose. "He isn't talking about victory. He's talking about suicide."

"Commander, why don't you tell us what you're thinking?"

"Certainly. Before we entered Freedom, I received extensive intel on our enemy from…a reliable source." The source was

Mittelman, and he'd barely caught himself before revealing the spymaster's name. "With the frigate, I'm not just targeting a weak ship, but a relatively inexperienced crew. After we destroy her, I will target another ship with a green crew. The more hulls we can account for, the faster Pegg's doubt will grow. By fragmenting his fleet, we'll force him to stand down."

Guerrero turned from her console again, and for once, her voice didn't shake at all. "Sir, we're ten seconds from entering effective firing range."

"Comply with the Commander's order, Moll," Rose said. "Or the deal's off."

"Fine," Moll spat, and vanished from the holotank.

"Thank you, Ms. Rose." Thatcher's eyes fell on his tactical officer. "Ortega, I hope you've already calculated a firing solution for that frigate."

"I have, sir."

"Then fire."

CHAPTER THIRTY-SIX

Aboard the *New Jersey*
Freedom System, Dupliss Region
Earth Year 2290

"FIRING PRIMARY."

The entire cruiser thrummed with the energy pouring out of her to lance across the void. Thatcher's holoscreen showed a realistic simulation of five other bright blue beams stemming from the other vessels comprising his main attack force.

Seconds later, an explosion replaced the frigate on his tactical display. It hadn't even managed to put up shields in time.

"Guerrero, relay the next targets to the battle group."

"Aye, Captain."

The frigate they'd just destroyed had not, in fact, contained the least experienced crew Reardon had. He'd selected it because another inexperienced crew piloted a corvette just beyond it, and a converted freighter filled with pirates also held formation nearby.

This time, his battle group split their fire between the two targets. As laserfire shot across the battlespace, shields finally flickered to life around most of Reardon's ships. *Pegg probably ordered them to conserve their energy until they needed shields.* But apparently he hadn't anticipated the inexperienced crew failing to react to the focused fire in time. Now, he was playing it safe by telling every ship that had shields to use them.

The freighter lacked shields, and its hull ruptured even faster than the frigate's. But the corvette's force field held longer than Thatcher had expected, with six powerful beams hammering down on it.

Then he saw them: two logistics ships lingering at the rear of the enemy formation, just close enough to feed energy to the corvette.

He was about to call out another target, one that was out of the logistics ships' range—when the entire Reardon formation shifted. Its left flank was snapping inward, stabbing with sapphire rays. All of them targeting the *Victorious*.

"Guerrero, tell the *Lightfoot* to get over there and bolster the destroyer's shields."

But even as he gave the order, the Sunder logistics ship started toward Moll's besieged command.

Guerrero seemed about to acknowledge the order, but he spoke over her. "Have the *Redpole* directionally jam as many of the ships targeting the *Victorious* as she can." *Redpole* was the eWar ship flying with his main attack force.

"Aye, sir." Then, Guerrero's body seemed to grow even more rigid, though Thatcher wouldn't have said that was possible. "Sir —the rest of Reardon's ships are closing in."

It was true. Pegg was tightening the noose, and even as he watched, the Reardon flank not targeting the *Victorious* unleashed a volley of missiles interspersed with lasers.

"Shields up, all ships!"

Guerrero distributed the order immediately, and to Frontier's credit, every ship put their shields up in time to intercept the incoming fire.

That served to deflect the missiles, whose explosive power dispersed across the energy fields of multiple ships. But it seemed the missiles' many targets had been chosen in the hopes of catching a crew unprepared, as Thatcher had with the frigate. The laserfire, however, all landed on the same target—the *Boxer*, Commander Frailey's command. Without a logistics ship there to support her, the shields spasmed violently, then went out.

No. "All ships target those firing on the *Boxer* with primaries!"

But it was too late. The beams hit the frigate's hull, drilling holes deep into her guts. She exploded.

Damn it. Though they'd only spoken a few times, Thatcher had grown fond of Frailey.

You can't protect everyone, Tad. His grandfather's words again.

"Ops, where's that flank?"

"The ships are still mustering at the Helio base, sir."

Even as Guerrero spoke, the Reardon ships that had taken out the *Boxer* switched to targeting the *Condor*, a Frontier corvette. Her shields shuddered for a few seconds, then fell. The lasers found her hull, and she went the way of Frailey's ship.

All the while, the *Victorious*' force field continued to quiver, kept on the brink of falling by the *Lightfoot*'s efforts.

CHAPTER THIRTY-SEVEN

Aboard the *New Jersey*
Freedom System, Dupliss Region
Earth Year 2290

"THE RESERVE AND OUTRIDER HAVE RALLIED AND ARE MOVING out from the Helio base to flank, sir."

"Excellent. Thank you, Guerrero." *If we can just hold things together a little longer, maybe there's a chance.*

Thatcher's eyepiece notified him of a call from Veronica Rose, and he snatched his comm from its holster on the side of his chair, thumbing the button to accept before letting it drop into its cradle once more.

"Yes?"

"Commander. I've been monitoring the battle from my office."

He resisted the urge to snap at his boss, to demand to know what she wanted. Behavior like that would soon be taken up by the crew.

"I just…" Rose cleared her throat. "It isn't enough for us to win this battle, Commander. We need to win with enough forces to hold Oasis, and to remain an attractive partner to Moll and the rest of his alliance. Frontier's longterm survival depends on it."

"I'm well aware of that, Ms. Rose." His voice sounded brittle to his own ears. *Keep it together.* "It's why I've been trying to secure a surrender from Pegg. Unfortunately, I believe he's just as aware of our predicament. He's pressuring us in exactly the way we've tried to pressure him. Which is why I need to focus on the engagement right now."

"Yes…I know. I'm sorry. I find it difficult to just sit here and monitor the battle, feeling completely powerless. But I'll let you get back to it. Good luck, Thatcher. I think I'll stop watching the engagement."

"That may be best." Thatcher plucked the comm from its holster once more and ended the call.

"Sir!" Guerrero choked out.

She said nothing else, apparently overcome with panic, but Thatcher saw the source of her distress clearly enough. Pegg's destroyer had finally advanced through the enemy formation, backed up by a logistics ship. Both vessels were positioned to cut off *Jersey* from her allies.

The *Eagle*'s primary laser shot out, slamming into the cruiser's shield and sending a cascade of rippling energy out from the impact point.

"Return fire with our primary, Ortega. Have the forward gunners target the destroyer's shield as well."

"Aye, sir."

The *Jersey*'s thick beam projected through the void, accompanied by multiple smaller, abbreviated rays. Thatcher called up a shield readout on his console and swallowed hard. Without a logistics ship of her own, the cruiser's shields were dropping fast.

His gaze flew back to the 3D tactical display beneath the readout. It held little to lessen his distress. The reserve was being intercepted by ships from Reardon's right flank, and on the opposite side of the engagement, the two forces were trading ships. The *Victorious* managed to take out an enemy cruiser, but a Frontier frigate soon followed. Now, Reardon was going after the *Lightfoot*, pushing it away from Moll's destroyer. If it fell out of range for supplementing the *Victorious'* shields, that could also prove disastrous for Frontier's fledgling alliance with Sunder. Hard to partner with a dead CEO.

Every friendly ship was occupied with the task of staying alive, with none available to help the *New Jersey*.

Guerrero found her voice again, though it came out as a low croak. "Shields down to thirty-five percent, sir."

"Acknowledged." For a moment, Thatcher marveled at how calm he sounded. None of this felt real. It was like a dream, or maybe a training simulation back in the academy. An interesting puzzle his instructors had devised for him to solve—if indeed they'd included the possibility of a solution at all. In war, some scenarios simply had no victory condition.

"Ten percent, sir." Guerrero sounded close to tears.

He knew she must be tortured by thoughts of her husband and children on the planet's surface, doomed to lifelong slavery, if not an early death.

But he couldn't concern himself with that right now. His mind ran faster than it ever had before, churning through variable after variable. A distracted part of him wondered whether this was a process that might produce a positive result, or simply the flailing of a terrified consciousness in the moments before death.

He pushed that aside as well, instead considering the enemy fleet's posture as well as that of his own fleet; the task each vessel was engaged in; Reardon's delicate position in the Dawn Cluster at large contrasted with their dominant position here in Freedom. What he knew from Mittelman about each enemy ship's crew, as well as Pegg himself. By all accounts, he was a bold man with unbridled ambition, but also a strong instinct for self-preservation. He was willing to enforce his upper hand mercilessly, when he had it, but he also knew to play conservatively if it served his best interests.

Last, Thatcher considered the battlespace as a whole. Even in a 3D environment, the flow of the engagement limited each ship's options. Where she could move, which hostile unit she might engage. Her options for defending herself.

The stillness in his CIC was absolute.

Then, Guerrero broke the silence. "Sir, our shields just went down."

Eagle stopped firing her primary a second later—in a one-on-one engagement, it was much more efficient to rely on missiles and autoturrets to rupture an armored hull.

Right on cue, two missiles departed the destroyer's tubes to hurtle across the void toward the *Jersey*. The cruiser's autoturrets took down one, but the other struck home, rocking her entire frame and throwing everyone in the CIC against their restraints.

Thatcher was about to order evasive action when the chief engineer contacted him.

"Go ahead, Ainsley."

"Sir, you can't move the ship."

"Why not?"

"That last missile screwed up one of the auxiliary thrusters. Its feed system got knocked out of calibration. Antimatter made it past the attenuating matrix and the magnetic storage rings. If we move now, there's a good chance it will trigger an annihilation. We'd be done for."

Thatcher found himself gripping his chair's armrests, his knuckles whitening. "How fast can you fix it?"

"Honestly, I don't know, sir. Devine and Jowers are headed there now."

On Thatcher's holoscreen, the *Eagle* loosed two more missiles.

CHAPTER THIRTY-EIGHT

Aboard the *New Jersey*
Freedom System, Dupliss Region
Earth Year 2290

"Come on!" Jowers roared from a few meters ahead.

With an effort of will, Devine forced his legs to move faster, a rattling steel toolbox gripped in each hand. *Guess I've been slacking off with PT.* It was hard to stay motivated with a boss like Commander Ainsley, who personally avoided exercise at all costs. But that was no excuse for Devine to do the same.

Technically, he outranked Tony Jowers, who shouldn't be shouting orders back at his superior. But this was no time to dwell on the chain of command. Right now, all that mattered was that they reach the *Jersey*'s bow section as fast as humanly possible.

Another missile struck home. The passageway bucked, and Devine found himself in midair for a fleeting moment, before coming down hard on his side. The toolbox in his left hand connected with his knee, sending pain shooting through his leg, but the other hit the deck hard. The latch popped open, and tools flew across the deck.

"Damn it. Come help me, Jowers."

"No. We have to go."

"*Come help me,* I said!"

Jowers tossed his head in frustration, but he ran back and begin scooping up the tools with Devine, helping him cram them back in the toolbox whatever way they would fit. *We might need one of these.* If they did, he doubted they'd have the time to run back here and collect them.

"Let's go," he said once all the tools had been stuffed inside, with the box's latch secured once more. Jowers grabbed his pair of toolboxes, and they dashed along the passageway as fast as their heavy metal loads would allow.

They raced toward one of the *Jersey's* port-side auxiliary thrusters. Not a critical ship component, under normal circumstances—but repairing it had become *very* critical when a missile had impacted the bow near it, which compressed the metal around the thruster and disrupted the emergency ejection system.

The ejection system served as a final defense against an internal antimatter leak. If every other failsafe malfunctioned, the computer would simply jettison the afflicted thruster, rather than risk a catastrophic explosion that would rip apart an entire section of the ship, if not the ship itself.

In the case of the auxiliary thruster, every failsafe but one had...well, failed. The feed system was knocked out of calibration, and the computer had shut it off, but not before a significant amount of antimatter had been injected into the positron conduit. The primary attenuating matrix had been breached, and so had two of the magnetic storage rings. Now, all that kept the antimatter at bay was the final magnetic casing, which was designed to keep the free-roaming positrons spinning around the thruster's internal housing until the whole apparatus could be ejected. Except, the ejection system was broken. The last failsafe wasn't made to contain the antimatter for this long, and even a single positron spiraling out of control could cause a cascade effect on the antimatter's stability. The result would be catastrophic.

"Shit," Jowers said from up ahead. He stood where the passageway turned right to run parallel to the *Jersey*'s port side.

Devine drew up beside him, panting. Then, his stomach clenched. The passage ahead was blocked off by a closed hatch.

"That last rocket must have blown the section open to space." Jowers stamped his foot, letting his toolkits fall to the deck, where they bounced roughly but didn't come open. "One of us has to suit up."

"I'll do it."

The deck engineer turned to study his face with wide eyes. "Seriously?"

"Didn't your whole family move to Dupliss?"

"Yeah. To the new colony on Marconi."

"Well, they'll want to see you again. I don't have anyone in the Dawn Cluster, and I doubt I'll ever get back to Venus. I'll go in."

Jowers' shoulders rose and fell as he seemed to take a deep breath. "I was wrong about the old man. You were right—he's the best thing that could have happened to the *Jersey*."

"Only if we take care of this thruster. Come on. Help me suit up."

They sprinted back to the last supply closet they'd passed and pulled out a pressure suit close to Devine's size. He stepped into it, and Jowers helped him fasten the many seals, checking them over as quickly as they could. Similarly equipped closets were distributed all throughout the *Jersey*'s exterior passageways. A hull breach could happen anywhere, after all.

At last, Devine stood near the sealed-off passageway, with Jowers at a control panel several meters away.

"Hit it."

Jowers punched the panel, and a second barrier descended

from the overhead, blocking him from view. This formed an impromptu airlock, and at once vents built into the bulkhead began sucking out all the air.

At last, the barrier blocking the section that was open to space retracted into the overhead. Devine stared at the tools at his feet. *What am I likely to need down there?*

He plucked up the toolbox with all the power wrenches, but that was probably wishful thinking. More likely, the missile had twisted the metal around the auxiliary thruster enough to make this a bigger job than loosening a few bolts.

He opened a second toolbox and took out a laser cutter, which he affixed to his belt. Then he jogged down the corridor toward where the damaged thruster waited.

The ship rocked again, throwing him forward. But before he could crash to the ground, the gravity failed. He smashed into the overhead, managing to grab a handle and steady himself in time to watch his toolbox hurtle down the corridor, passing the thruster access before ricocheting off a bulkhead and careening even farther out of reach.

"Damn it." *Well, I doubt those wrenches would have done me much good anyway.*

He pushed off from the handle to send himself floating forward, catching another one as he drew level with the damaged thruster.

Game time. He drew a deep breath and keyed open the thruster access, reading the proper code off his eyepiece, from a message Ainsley had sent him as he and Jowers had sped through the *Jersey.*

He drew back to let the hatch's hydraulics push it open, then poked his head inside.

Oh, Lord.

The thruster's inner casing was a twisted mess—warped enough to turn the fact that no annihilation had taken place into convincing evidence for the existence of God. To an engineer, anyway.

Then again, the fact the *Jersey* was still intact seemed like evidence enough.

Devine got to work, using the laser to cut through one of three places that seemed to be holding the thruster fast. Sweat dripped from his chin onto his faceplate as the beam slowly separated the twisted knot of metal, which reminded him of a bird's nest. *Come on. Come on.*

He finished cutting…and nothing happened. He'd hoped to see the casing shift outward, or at least some sign he was making progress. But the thruster stayed exactly where it was.

Next one. He rotated in the cramped compartment, until his head was roughly where his feet had been. He activated the laser once more.

When he finished cutting this time, the thruster did shift forward, and if he hadn't been working in a vacuum he was sure there'd be an ominous groan of metal. But the casing only moved an inch.

For a moment, he eyed the final spot that needed cutting. *If that doesn't do it…*

But he couldn't think about that. He rotated himself once more and activated the laser.

Halfway through, the entire casing shot forward, and a thrill ran through his chest.

Then, it stopped, after moving just a few more inches.

That was it. There was nowhere else to cut.

He raised a hand toward the panel on the side of his helmet, to tell his comm to contact Ainsley. But what point was there? There was nothing the chief engineer could do from the main engineering deck. The ejection system had already been engaged automatically, and it had failed.

So had Devine. Right now, he was *Jersey*'s only chance to avoid becoming so much floating shrapnel. And he'd failed.

He moved without thinking, at first unsure what he was doing. His hand found the hatch's handle in the passageway outside, and he pulled it shut.

Wow. I do believe I've lost my marbles.

Despite that, he planted his feet on the hatch, wedging his back against the thruster's casing. And he pushed.

For several moments, nothing happened.

What do you think you're doing, Devine? Do you think you're actually going to push this thing out of here?

But he continued to strain, ignoring the sensation that his spine might snap in two at any moment.

"*Agh!*" The grunt filled his helmet, and it took him a moment to realize he'd produced it. "*Aghhh!*"

The casing shifted. Just an inch, maybe less, but it shifted.

He shoved harder, stretching his body between the thruster casing and the hatch, ignoring his fear the hatch would simply pop open.

Millimeter by millimeter, the thruster began to scrape outward.

Then, without warning, it left the *Jersey* altogether, leaving a gaping hole where the apparatus had been.

Devine scrabbled for purchase, his hands grasping for something to stop his momentum, anything. But there was nothing to grab onto. Engineers weren't meant to climb inside thruster compartments to push thrusters out of the craft.

So he followed the thing into the void of space, cartwheeling end over end, just another piece of debris.

CHAPTER THIRTY-NINE

Aboard the *New Jersey*
Freedom System, Dupliss Region
Earth Year 2290

"THE THRUSTER HAS BEEN EJECTED, SIR," COMMANDER AINSLEY
said. The chief engineer sounded breathless but relieved. "We're
out of the woods."

*Where the thruster's concerned, maybe. There's still the
destroyer bombarding us.* "Acknowledged, Commander. And
good work." He thumbed his comm to end the conversation.

While engineering had scrambled to rid the *Jersey* of the
thruster, Thatcher had been forced to rely on autoturrets to
defend against incoming missiles from the *Eagle*, supplemented
by manual point defense fire from his gunner crews. Only two
missiles had gotten through, but that was two too many, and it
would only take one or two more well-placed Hellborns to make
sure Thatcher's first command was also his last.

He knew the missiles were Hellborns, because he'd ordered
Ainsley to try hacking them, and it hadn't worked. Defeat stared
back at Thatcher from the tactical display on his holoscreen, and

he knew that if he didn't do something drastic, it would claim him.

But his mind had continued to churn during the forced stand-still, and he had an idea.

"Ops, order *Squall* and *Redpole* to draw toward the center of the engagement—toward the *Eagle*. The moment they're in range to affect the destroyer, I want them to blanket the battle-space with omnidirectional jamming bursts."

To her credit, Guerrero didn't hesitate. "Aye, sir." She raised a hand to her ear and began to relay his orders to the electronic warfare ships.

The enemy logistics ship kept the destroyer's shields healthy, but during the struggle Thatcher had tracked the evolving flow of the engagement, as options were closed to each actor while new ones opened up.

He'd read about rare naval captains of old with the uncanny ability to anticipate enemy movements—to get inside their heads, using only their intuition and seamanship to do so. That had been incredible enough in a 2D environment; the open sea. Now Thatcher would need to replicate it in 3D.

To carry out Thatcher's bidding, the eWar ships didn't have far to go. Less than two minutes after he'd given the order, they triggered their bursts, and his tactical display went blank, cut off from all sensor data. An instant later, it refreshed with the last known positions of each vessel.

"Nav, take us on a course trending toward the *Squall*, now. Tactical, continue firing the primary at the destroyer's last known location, and prepare to update your firing solution to track the *Eagle*'s movement."

Ortega looked up from his console and blinked at Thatcher. "But sir—how will we track her without sensor data?"

"She'll be where I say she is. For now, continue firing on that spot, but prepare to update according to a projected course I'll send you. Have gunner crews stand by to add their fire."

He was working on the projected course now. Probably, he should have gotten Sullivan involved in this process, but there was no time to have the Nav officer check over his calculations. Instead, he'd have to draw on what he remembered from every astrogation course he'd ever taken, knowing that failure would mean death at worst and the loss of his crew's trust at best.

One thing he could be sure of: the enemy logistics ship had almost certainly stopped feeding power to the destroyer. Tracking a receiver array with a microwave beam was a delicate process, and the targeting required constant updating. While Ortega only needed to hit the destroyer anywhere on its hull, the logistics ship would need to aim for a tiny part of it. *Next to impossible, without updated sensor data.*

Without the help of the logistics ship, the destroyer's shields would fail. Once they did, Pegg would begin evasive maneuvers.

The question was, where would he move? Thatcher thought he had the answer, but there would be no do-over. If he guessed incorrectly, he and his crew would likely die.

"Sending you the projected course now, Ortega." Thatcher tapped at his console to transmit his calculations. "Assume the destroyer is accelerating as fast as she can, using one hundred percent of her engine power. Nav, prepare to change course to give chase, and Helm, bring us up to one hundred percent as well."

The three officers mumbled their acknowledgments, so intent they were on their respective tasks. Normally, Thatcher would rebuke such sloppy form, but right now they were welcome to behave in whatever way helped them concentrate.

Thatcher had done what he could to get inside Pegg's head—to see the engagement as he saw it. He'd needed to factor in the fact that Thatcher's move with the eWar ships would likely come as a surprise. That limited Pegg's reaction time.

What would Thatcher have done in Pegg's position, with his

sensors fogged and laserfire coming from nowhere to finish off his shields?

Oasis. Pegg certainly wouldn't fly toward the *Jersey*, and Thatcher doubted he'd fly deeper into the battlespace, either. Instead, he would flee toward the one thing keeping Reardon Interstellar safe: the planet they held.

"Ortega, I want you to stop firing the primary and instead fire a Hellborn in Barrage Mode." Barrage Mode was an innovation Thatcher had arrived at with Commander Ainsley after the Olent engagement. Now, instead of having to separately reprogram each missile to repeat the trick he'd used then, every Hellborn on the *Jersey* could be switched over to the new mode before firing. "We will build up a barrage of four missiles, accelerating to catch up to our Hellborns before firing the next."

"But sir...that would mean firing in the direction of the planet. If we miss..."

Thatcher nodded. Normally, he wouldn't condone anyone questioning his orders, but Ortega's fear was legitimate. No one wanted nuclear warheads exploding within the Oasis' atmosphere. "According to Commander Ainsley, we should be able to divert the missiles remotely. But in case we can't, Guerrero, I want you to order the two reserve corvettes to chase the *Eagle* as well, so that they're in position to neutralize those missiles."

"Aye, sir."

The first Hellborn left the missile tube, sending a tremor through the ship that vibrated Thatcher in his chair. A tense silence had descended over the CIC, each officer bent to their task as the *Jersey* hurtled through the sensor fog after her quarry. The two warships were in a race to be the first to overcome the omnidirectional jamming—the first to react to whatever new reality had gripped the battlespace.

The second Hellborn launched. Then, minutes later, the third.

Thatcher's gaze was glued to his holoscreen. The tactical

display program was smart enough to track the destroyer's projected course across the void, representing its expected position as a ghostly, segmented outline of the vessel. Once it regained the benefit of sensor data, it would update with its actual position.

The fourth Hellborn launched.

At last, Guerrero spoke, her voice shaking, but this time with excitement instead of uncertainty. "Sir, the *Squall* is feeding us updated sensor data. The *Eagle* is exactly where you said she would be."

Thatcher took no time to celebrate the victory. "Forward that sensor data to all four Hellborns, Guerrero. They'll need it to zero in on the target. Helm, begin deceleration."

"Aye, sir," came the reply from both officers.

The *Eagle* had also regained its bearings, it seemed. Her gunner crews sprang to life, batteries spitting secondary lasers to intercept the *Jersey*'s ordnance. One Hellborn went down. Then, a second.

Thatcher's heart sank. It seemed certain now that they would intercept a third, and maybe the fourth. Even if they didn't get them all, one missile wasn't likely to do the damage Thatcher knew would be needed to end this.

"Ortega—"

But he fell silent as both missiles slipped through the laserfire to slam into the *Eagle*'s stern. The first blew open a broad section of hull, and the other took out one of the destroyer's two primary thrusters.

She's mine. For the first time since he took command of the *New Jersey*, his CIC crew bust into cheering.

He had no choice but to cut it short. "Resume full acceleration, Helm. Guerrero, contact Pegg."

"Aye, sir."

Seconds later, Pegg's bald head gleamed in the holotank. He'd taken his sunglasses off to reveal small gray eyes, which were about as wide as they could go and filled with rage. He said nothing.

"We have you, Pegg. I'll extend my offer one last time before I turn your ship to scrap. Surrender and depart this system with every Reardon ship, leaving the surviving pirates to us. Never return."

"Fine," Pegg spat.

"Give the order to disengage now. You will keep your ship where she is until all your other ships have left. Show me one sign of going back on your word, and this will be your last day."

He signaled for Guerrero to cut off the transmission. And when Pegg disappeared from the holotank, Thatcher leaned back in his chair, exhaling slowly as the tension leaked from his body.

His worst fear hadn't been realized. The Xanthic had not arrived to back up Reardon.

That was both a relief and a worry. If they hadn't struck here, it might mean they were planning for something bigger.

He simply didn't know. The Xanthic's motives seemed just as alien as they did.

CHAPTER FORTY

On Oasis Helio Base 5
Freedom System, Dupliss Region
Earth Year 2290

"TAKE A LOOK AT THIS, TAD." VERONICA ROSE SWIVELED THE
holoscreen till it faced him. "It's a sensor suite upgrade for a
brand-new type of sensor. Apparently Nutronics is the first to
offer it in the Dawn Cluster."

"Hmm?" Thatcher said, blinking. "Oh."

He'd been lost in thought about his recent interrogations of
pirates who Mittelman said were connected with those that had
fought against Captain Vaughn alongside the Xanthic warship.

Every one of them had claimed that no pirate had an alliance
with the Xanthic. According to their version of events, no one
among the crews of the pirate ships that had fought the *Jersey*
had even known the alien ship was with them in the gas giant's
cloud. It simply rose up to join the engagement on their side, and
had disappeared the moment the *Jersey* had fled. They didn't
mean it had left the system—according to every account
Thatcher heard, it had literally vanished.

Of course, these were all second-hand accounts, and if just one or two of them had claimed these things, he would have dismissed them out of hand. But other than a few errant details, the stories he heard were all remarkably similar. It seemed the story of the Xanthic's appearance had affected the pirate world just as much as it would affect the rest of the Cluster, if and when it got out.

Thatcher studied the display Rose was showing him, reflecting on the fact she'd called him "Tad" again. He didn't remember when that had started, but he was sure he didn't like it. "A polarization sensor?"

She nodded. "For detecting antimatter engines, even after they've left the system."

He narrowed his eyes and read over the Nutronics marketing copy. "Not sure what the use case would be. Unless it can match antimatter emissions to the ship that produced them, which I doubt. Nearly every system we pass through is bound to be criss-crossed with antimatter trails."

"What about in Contested Systems? Chasing down pirates and the like?"

"Most pirate ships still run on fission."

"True. But this could still be useful to have."

He shrugged, allowing himself a brief smile. "If I don't have to sacrifice anything for it, and Frontier's willing to pay for it, then I'll sign off on it."

Rose smiled back. "For the *New Jersey*? After her performance against Reardon? Yes, I do believe Frontier's willing to pay for it."

He nodded and turned back to studying his own holoscreen, but not before he caught the prideful grins from Ainsley and Devine at the CEO's praise. Not Candle, though. His gaze remained glued to his own holoscreen as he reviewed potential upgrades, as stoic as ever.

They'd picked up Jimmy Devine after the battle, kept alive

by his pressure suit. The thruster he'd successfully dislodged had exploded less than a minute later, but he'd managed to push himself away from it, making it far enough that none of the resultant debris found him. Thatcher knew the hours the lad had spent hurtling through the void couldn't have been comfortable.

To conserve power in those circumstances, the suit only kept its occupant warm enough to avoid freezing to death—which was still pretty cold. But Devine had survived with a couple hours of oxygen to spare, and since then he'd seemed more chipper than ever.

How could he not, with the praise getting heaped on him? The young engineer's actions had saved his ship, and his crewmates and superiors had taken every opportunity to make sure Devine knew it. Thatcher had included him in today's meeting to provide context on what had happened with the auxiliary thruster, and to offer his input on any changes they made to the *Jersey*'s engineering plant.

He just hoped Devine was strong enough to take all this praise without getting sloppy. He'd seen too many good officers grow ineffective as compliment after compliment swelled their heads.

Of course, since the battle for Oasis the entire crew seemed to walk with a spring in their step. Five pirate ships had been taken in the wake of Reardon's departure. Between the captured vessels and the scrap salvaged from ships during the engagement, there was plenty of prize money to go around, even divided between ten ships. Simon Moll had declined the offer of prize money for his crews, as a gesture of goodwill at the start of Sunder's partnership with Frontier.

"I think we should reduce our complement of repair drones by half," Thatcher said after playing around with the Nutronics outfitting tool for around twenty minutes. "If we shift Capacitor Module C to where Drone Bay B is now, we can place a second missile tube on our starboard side." This was the beauty of the

Gladius combat system's modularity: it allowed a captain to adapt his system to the conditions he expected to face. The challenge lay in determining what those conditions would actually be.

Candle looked up from his holoscreen to meet Thatcher's eyes across the conference table. "That will make *Jersey* more vulnerable."

"Only if we're unaccompanied by logistics ships. But it seems we're to play a more defensive role, going forward. If we're to honor our commitment to our new partners, we'll need to focus on locking down Dupliss. Which makes it likely we'll have support ships on hand at any given time." Thatcher glanced at Rose.

"Tad is right. It's impossible to predict the future, but defending Dupliss looms large on our agenda. Of course, controlling the entire region with just the ships we have is another matter altogether. Still no word from UNC on whether they're planning to share nanofab tech, or let us exceed their limit on corporate military size."

Thatcher wondered whether the UNC would bother replying to Rose's request. As for Candle's comment on reducing the *Jersey*'s repair drones, Thatcher didn't begrudge him the input. On the contrary: he wanted an XO who was willing to give his honest opinion. There would inevitably be times when Thatcher *was* wrong about something, and if no one pointed it out to him, it could doom his ship.

What surprised Thatcher the most was Candle's decision to remain aboard the *New Jersey* as XO. Rose had offered him his own command in the *Charger*, but Candle had declined.

That had cheered Thatcher...until the next time he'd spoken to Hans Mittelman.

"Harden yourself against flattery, Commander," the chief intelligence officer had said. "Remember that anyone at all might be another corp's spy."

A smiling Nutronics employee wheeled in a tray filled with refreshments, and they each accepted a tea or coffee while helping themselves to the offered biscuits. It wasn't much, but still a nice gesture, and aboard a Helio base the snack came close to luxury.

They took a break from developing the *Jersey*'s new loadout to enjoy the cookies and beverages. Thatcher leaned back in his seat, studying the bulkhead above his XO's head as he lost himself in thought about the recent engagement—what he could have done better, and what could have gone worse, if he'd been less fortunate. He felt no pressure to break the silence with chitchat.

"Oh!" Rose sat straighter in her seat to fish her comm from her pocket, placing it on the tabletop. "I forgot. Simon Moll is making his first address to the Dawn Cluster."

She connected her comm to speakers set into the bulkheads around the room, and Moll's booming voice sounded all around them.

"—opposed to our cause. Ultimately, their opposition is irrelevant. Sunder Incorporated will continue to exhibit the excellence that is our hallmark. We have decades of successful military ops under our belt, and we've partnered with some of the Dawn Cluster's most effective corps. If your corp is surrounded by enemies and lacking the ability to defend itself, get in touch. We are willing to extend the stability we have created in the northwest to any corp willing to work with us."

"Wait a second," Devine said, looking around at his superiors. "What is he proposing, exactly?"

Rose opened her mouth to answer, but before she could, a strident beeping replaced Moll's voice.

Thatcher recognized that tone: it signified a priority transmission, coming through the CEO's comm.

She disconnected the device from the bulkhead speakers and brought it to her ear. "Veronica Rose."

Her face whitened as she listened, and her eyes met Thatcher's. Then she terminated the call without saying anything else to the caller, leapt to her feet, and stuffed the comm back into her pocket.

"We have to go. *Now.* Oasis is under attack."

Thatcher's eyes widened. "That's impossible. We would have been notified the moment a warship entered the system."

"It's not an attack from a warship. It's the Xanthic. They're attacking from under the ground, just like they did on Earth."

GLOSSARY OF DAWN CLUSTER CORPORATIONS

Frontier Security

CEO: Veronica Rose

CIO: Hans Mittelman

Frontier is a security firm that prides itself on upholding American values. Founded in Earth Year 2259 by Rear Admiral Gregory Rose, his daughter Veronica now runs the company. Her stated intention is to stay true to her father's vision.

Currently, Frontier forms part of the Oasis Protectorate, a conglomerate formed for the purpose of servicing and protecting American colonies located throughout the Dawn Cluster's Dupliss Region.

Reardon Interstellar

CEO: Ramon Pegg

Founded in Earth Year 2210, Reardon was one of the first PMCs (private military companies) to offer its services in the Dawn Cluster, in response to a growing threat from pirates based in the Contested Regions. Reardon identifies as an American company, but has also accepted contracts from various US trading partners, along with countries that have less-certain relationships with the USA, including China and Russia. In response to media inquiries concerning these latter contracts, Reardon CEOs have typically pointed out that, with the rise of the United Nations and Colonies, war between nations has become virtually extinct. It is therefore foolish to turn down any contracts.

Reardon has consistently denied rumors alleging the company has engaged in hot-system skirmishes against other Dawn Cluster corporations. Reardon forms part of the Oasis Protectorate, however at the time of writing its position within the Protectorate has been called into question, with allegations being forwarded by multiple interested parties that the company has been consorting with pirates.

Sunder Incorporated

CEO: Simon Moll

Sunder holds the distinction of being the first PMC to accept a security contract within the Dawn Cluster. While headquartered in Candor, a Cluster Region, the company draws its employees mostly from European countries and colonies, primarily German and Swedish. Sunder was founded in 2208 by a former UNC dreadnought commander, Captain Patrick Moen, and the company has only had two CEOs since its inception—Moen and Simon Moll.

In the 2250s, Spanish biographer Luis Borges made the claim that Moen and Moll were the same person. As evidence, Borges highlighted Moll's lack of a documented past before his involvement with the company, the fact there is nothing to indicate the

Sunder CEOs have ever met, and a number of physical similarities between the two men. Borges claimed that Moll underwent extensive cosmetic surgery to change his identity, though he did not advance any theory of why Moll would go to these efforts.

In recent decades, Borges's claims have been dismissed as fringe conspiracy theory, since in order for them to be true, Moll would have to be in excess of 160 years old—twenty-seven years older than the eldest human being ever documented.

A NOTE ON DAWN CLUSTER CARTOGRAPHY

In the Dawn Cluster, cardinal directions are used for ease of reference, with the black hole at the galaxy's center acting as a "north star."

Terms such as north, south, east, and west are meaningful because of the Cluster's layout. While star systems *are* distributed along the Z-axis, with a maximum spread of 13.781 light years, the Cluster's X- and Y-axes are much longer, at 105.134 light years and 81.240 light years respectively.

ACKNOWLEDGMENTS

Thank you to my Alpha Team, who have been reading this book since its earliest stage and who've provided substantial feedback along the way, which helped me develop the story with my readers' desires foremost in mind. They are Rex Bain, Sheila Beitler, Bruce Brandt, Colin Oliver, Jeff Rudolph, and Ben Varela.

Thank you to my proofreading team, who helped eliminate scores of spelling and grammar issues. I take full responsibility for any mistakes that remain :) My proofreaders are Rex Bain, Sheila Beitler, Bruce Brandt, and Jeff Rudolph.

A special thank you to my Patreon supporters at the Space Fleet Admiral level. Your support helps me to package my books as professionally as possible while staying true to what my readers like best about my books. My Space Fleet Admiral patrons are Brian Loeung, David Middleton, Lawrence Tate, and Michael Van De Hey. Thank you so much.

Thank you also to Patreon supporters Rex Bain, Richard Gunn, Alex Hamilton, Christian Kallias, John A Koenig III, Daniel

Mabry, Jason Pennock, Wynand Pretorius, Bill Scarborough, John Tava, Ben Varela, and Jerry Winiarski.

Thank you to Jason Carayanniotis and Chris Evans for helping me flesh out the details for how some of the technology in the book works.

Thank you to Tom Edwards for creating such stunning cover art, as always.

Thank you to my family - Mom, Dad, and Danielle - your support means everything.

Thank you to the people who read my stories, write reviews, and help spread the word. I couldn't do this without you.

Made in the USA
Middletown, DE
25 September 2019